GIFTS OF GRACE

CYNTHIA BOWEN FLOYD

outskirts
press

Outskirts Press, Inc.
http://www.outskirtspress.com

Paperback ISBN: 978-1-9772-3938-9
Hardback ISBN: 978-1-9772-3514-5

Cover Photo © 2021 www.gettyimages.com. All rights reserved - used with permission.

Bible source: NIV Life Application Study Bible Copyright 2011 by Zondervan

Outskirts Press and the "OP" logo are trademarks belonging to Outskirts Press, Inc.

PRINTED IN THE UNITED STATES OF AMERICA

As I am riding down the east coast highway, life seems perfect; well almost. As I look out the passenger window, I can close my eyes and remember our wedding ceremony as if it were just yesterday. Has 7 years really passed us by? My mom is a stickler for details and etiquette, which can drive me utterly insane at times; but with every single detail of my wedding, her attention to details were perfect. The cake was beautiful in its simplicity with 4 tiers of white layers bordered in black ribbon and topped with a single red rose. Our wedding was performed in a simple, rustic chapel deep in the North Carolina mountains complete with surrounding cabins for our out of town visitors that came for our wedding. A small stream with a quiet trickle of water ran through the expanse of the cabins and provided the perfect peaceful background needed for those of us dealing with a case of the nerves. I chose October for the month of my wedding because all of the rich, lavish and vibrant green leaves of the trees from the Summer have now changed to a wonderful arrangement of yellow, gold, red and orange leaves that completely transform the entire landscape. It is in the month of October, that nature starts to settle in for a long winter nap; but oh how beautiful as nature gets ready for this transition. She (Nature) almost quietly changes her mood, from the thick, blanket of stifling heat (found in the South) to the quiet, peaceful and cool evenings, that I love so much about the Fall of the year. I can still remember standing with nervous trepidation and anticipation with my father at the end of the aisle. I grasp my father's hand tightly and we share a moment only between the two of us; my dad doesn't give me the father-daughter speech, he only whispers "I love you" and with tears in both of our eyes, we start the walk into my new life. I purposefully avoid Adam's eyes because I know that our time will come; this walk is with and for me and my dad. And when I unclasp my dad's hand, it is then that I hold Adams hand and I look into his eyes and I know; this is completely right.

We had always wanted children and not surprisingly I found myself pregnant within our first year of marriage. By this time, we had purchased a house together and I began working on the nursery, little by little preparing myself for our baby's birth. As soon as it was possible, we found out the sex of the baby and we found out it would be a little boy. Of course, my dad thought that it should be a surprise because in his mind and as he so eloquently states, "There are not many surprises in this life." The nursery was painted in vanilla crème with a border of deeply rich blue elephants and hardwood floors complete with thick Victorian rich rugs. As we had a couple of false alarms, I woke up that January night with awful cramping and decided I would wait it out a bit; just to see if this were again a false alarm. I tossed and turned for an hour or so and rolled out of the bed to try and maneuver my way to the kitchen for a cold glass of water. Why am I so thirsty? It was then that I noticed the spotting on my gown and felt the water running down the insides of my legs. Had my water broken? Surely that must be it but why am I spotting? We telephoned our doctor to let him know that my water had broken and I was spotting and he told Adam that he would meet us at the hospital.

My labor was intense and unrelenting but all of this was forgotten as Abel Nathaniel Morese made his debut at just around 4:00 a.m. the next morning. I thought I knew what love was; but I had no idea until I held this blessing called Abel. I really don't think that Adam's feet touched the floor, he was a happy daddy. I said a silent prayer of thanks to God above for this blessing and felt totally complete. This blessing; this joy grew into a delightful, mischievous little boy who could drive you to the edge of insanity only to pull you back and warm your heart with an affectionate hug or a kiss! Very bright and inquisitive, he loved for me or his dad to read to him every day and this most often occurred at his bedtime. His favorite story in the Bible was of Noah's Ark and we had a huge storybook complete with pictures that we read to him quite often. My mom and dad introduced me at an early age to Jesus, and I was determined to follow that tradition with Abel. He loved the idea that God saved Noah, his family and the animals but grew quite sad and pensive whenever he thought of those that opted not to believe Noah or God and had perished in the flood.

Abel loved all of his grandparents, but had an especially strong bond with my mother and insisted that "Grammie come and stay with us" at least once or twice a month. My mom made the stories that Abel loved from the Bible storybook come alive and make complete and perfect sense to our 5 year old. He fought the battle with David against Goliath, the giant and listened with pure rapture as she told of Moses leading the Israelites to safety through the parting of the Red Sea only to have the Red Sea "crush" the bad guys.

Summertime for me always meant the summers off

but for this particular summer, I opted as a teacher to teach a collegiate honors class for 4 weeks during the summer. Summers off with Abel always meant playing outside in his playhouse which he had aptly renamed his "tool shed" as his father also had one, complete with a make-believe tool bench and all the "necessary" tools needed; children's hammer, nails, screwdrivers and such. We had decided to purchase a pool when Abel was around 4 years and took every precaution with safety; even enrolling Abel in a swimmers classes at the local YMCA. Abel loved the pool and spent many happy hours in the pool; but it was always with an adult at the pool side, no exceptions to this rule. Abel was a gifted swimmer; and as I think back to those days, I can see just how very much he was the image of Adam. He had a stubborn curly mass of blonde locks, large liquid brown eyes and a very nice array of freckles that speckled his tanned chubby cheeks.

As I sit here, lost in my own thoughts, I study Adam as he drives. Gone are the easy readily visible laugh lines that surrounded his soft eyes; now they have been replaced by stern, deep lines that are surprisingly deeply etched into his handsome face. A feeble attempt at conversation between the two of us is only met with polite and vague responses. I continue; lost in my thoughts. Why did I take that job for the summer? I should have been home with my Abel; enjoying him, loving him. How could we have known that would be the last summer we had with our Abel.....And the last summer of us?

I can never truly recall all the details of that day after Abel's accident. I can tell you what I was wearing that morning to class, I could tell you how the weather was that morning; I could tell you details of my life on THAT day BEFORE the accident but not after...But I can still hear my mother's scream, the urgency and dread of that scream, "Noooooo! Oh God, no! Not my Abel!" I had just walked in the front door and had finished my class for the day and I dropped my book satchel on my arm, books in my hand, and an iced tea in the other and ran to the side door, only to find my mother waist deep in our swimming pool, turning Abel over on his back and pulling him over to the patio side of the pool. I couldn't speak and I felt frozen in time; frozen with fear. Until I heard my mother scream "Anna call 911 and get them on the phone NOW!" When someone you love dies, I firmly believe that it is truly so painful that your mind will completely block out certain aspects in order to protect its integrity. EMS arrived only to begin working on Abel immediately. And for 40 minutes of that time, I seized to breathe, think or exist. My gift from God, one of my greatest joys in the world was now gone.

I vaguely remember Abel's visitation as my brain was still trying to understand that he was gone while trying to steady itself before it plummeted into the abyss of insanity. Insanity where my grief wraps around me such as a python only then to squeeze the very life from me. My doctor had ordered a prescription of Valium to help with coping, but it only left me numb and lifeless. Many of our friends and family came to the visitation and while their attempts at sympathy and understanding was so appreciated; it felt awkward and uncomfortable. How do you comfort a grieving mother? I truly think there are no words known in the English language that can assuage the feeling of loss; absolutely none.

Adam did not attend his son's visitation and did not view his child's body. He absolutely refused and holed himself up in his den looking at photographs and watching videos and trying to numb himself with the very best bourbon in our cabinets. I stayed with Abel at the funeral home because in my peculiar reasoning, I assumed that he would be scared by himself at night! Scared!? My child was obviously not in this body any longer and I was worried that he might be scared!? How completely irrational is that? And so I stayed and slept on the couch where his body lay in respite for those 2 long nights sobbing with an occasional glimpse into the room by one of the attendants to check on me. "Why God? Why Abel? Why didn't you take one of those unworthy, hateful, sadistic pedophiles or those murderers; the murderers that take a precious life and in the process, ruin an entire family's life...? Why God?"

As we are now driving home from our vacation, I know in my heart that this was our last effort, our last attempt at patching the big hole that continues to grow, rip and separate us since Abel's death. Abel's death has changed both of us, leaving in its wake two very cynical, unhappy people that no longer believe in a loving God; a God that Abel loved so very much. My mother and Adam's mother have been wonderful, but I'm thinking that maybe they see the writing on the wall, just as we do. My mom, although heartbroken, takes comfort in knowing that Abel is in Heaven with my daddy and that she does have the promise of seeing them both again one day. I do feel guilty because it is my mom that I take my rage out on; my rage with God. I sometimes cringe inward at some of the comments that I've made to her..."Mom, I've lost a child! A child that did nothing wrong, but be a child and God took him from me. What did I do to God to make him take my child away?? An innocent child!!"

As we pull into our driveway, I still feel the tinge of homesickness for our lives before the accident, before God decided he wanted to take my Abel from me. As we unpack from our trip, check our messages on our home phone, and get our house in order for our week to begin tomorrow, I admit I feel a twinge of nostalgia for what we had; what we've lost and what could have been.

Adam is working on emails in his office and I'm ready for bed. I sit on the edge of the bed exhausted; physically, emotionally and spiritually; totally exhausted. As I lie back on my pillow, the tears come and as hard as I try, they will not stop their flow. My mom frequents the local Christian bookstore and had picked up a couple of books for me before our vacation. Needless to say they were packed but were left in the suitcase the entire trip. One of the books is a devotional that is enclosed in a beautiful leather binding with the inscription; "Jesus". I am still mad at God/Jesus and want absolutely no part of knowing Him and understanding the scripture or man's interpretation of why bad things happen in life. I can feel the books at the edge of the bed; reminding me of just how mad I am with God. I have no interest in reading His Word or trying to procure any understanding of His Word and I sit up in the bed and pick up the books and fling them across the room where they land with a loud thud on the floor beneath the window. I then manage albeit fitfully to fall asleep; but it is a sleep filled with terrors; with my last images of Abel. But then I wake up; wide awake and it's 2:30 a.m. Wait!? What is that light in the room? I attempt to cover my eyes at first from the pain of the glare, but then I slowly lower my hands to look at the light again. Am I dreaming? There is a figure at the end of my bed and the figure glows with a white almost tangible light! I stare in silence for several seconds only to have the silence broken with a soft, gentle voice calling my name..."Anna, it is I and I am here for you." "Excuse me, you are here for me? Who are you?" "I am the One that your Abel loves and I am the One that your Abel is with now. Your Abel asks that I take you to him." Is this real? Have I completely become unhinged? The scales of reason have finally toppled over the edge to the brink of insanity! Well, dreaming or not, I still would love to see Abel! I stood up at the side of the bed and this Being, full of light offers His hand to me and we are then outside of my bedroom and moving very fast upward through a dark tunnel filled with sporadically shooting light beams. "I'm afraid! Where are we going?" "Do not be afraid Anna. I am He and although you do not know this place, this place is where your Abel lives with Me." My mind was racing! What's going on? Admittedly while I was mad at God, I knew in an instant that because Abel was with this Being, He must be Jesus! "Are you Jesus?" "I AM."

In the next instant, we were standing in a field of beautifully green plush grass, sporadically covered with the richest most luxurious colors I have ever seen within flowers; bright and bold burgundy's, golden yellows, periwinkle blues, blue topaz, blood reds and rich deep purples. If this was "Heaven" and where Abel lived, I knew that he loved this place. Abel loved the outdoors; in fact anything that had to do with the outdoors was his idea of a perfect and wonderful day. Nothing inside or he quickly became bored! As I looked at Jesus within the realms of Heaven, I could sense a feeling of love; of warmth and true kindness that permeated His entire being. Everything felt familiar to me in this place. I had always explicitly trusted my mother in all matters, in everything, so why should I not have trusted her when she told me that Abel was in Heaven with Jesus.

"Anna I love you and I have always been with you. I know that you have many questions for Me, but lets go and see Abel first. I then turned around and Abel was standing within 2 feet of me and we were alone. Abel looked as he always had, head full of curly hair, big brown eyes, but best of all; Abel was glowing with happiness. With a smile on his face, he exclaimed "Oh mom, I'm so glad that you could come. Have you met Jesus? He takes good care of me, please don't worry about me." I could feel the dam break and my eyes fill with tears and the sobbing began; sobbing because I missed my boy but also so grateful that he was well and okay and most of all; happy! I fell to my knees and Abel ran into my arms and stayed there for awhile, while I enjoyed the relief of shedding the anger, resentment and the bitterness that I had felt since he left us. And in its stead; happiness, peace, and serenity came to live and reside within me and I welcomed all of them. This didn't feel like a dream.....not a dream at all! Abel's sweet wide eyed grin belied a deep concern as he said "Mommy, how are you and daddy doing? I know that you miss me and I missed you when I first came here but Jesus talks to me an awful lot, mommy. He explains things to me. Hey mommy, did you know that Jesus is my Father too? He spends A LOT of time with all of the children and he tells all of us that Heaven is our home now. Sometimes I talk with Jesus by myself and He told me that one day, you and daddy will live with me in Heaven too!" And with that he jumped into my arms again but this time sending both of us falling back into the grass laughing. Oh I had forgotten how good it felt to laugh; one of the simple joys of laughter. Sometimes Death himself can take your smile, joy or laugh away with him when he goes but never permanently....Death doesn't have that much power!

As I held my little boy, the pain, the hurt, the bitterness, and the grief of the last several months seemed to ebb away. I felt such tremendous love, serenity, happiness and peace in this Place; Heaven. Abel's sweet wide eyed grin, although he tried, did not hide concern as he said softly "Mommy, I am worried about you and daddy? I've missed you so much mommy but Jesus told me that we would be together again, and I totally trust Him." "Abel, I have missed you so...." And I couldn't finish the sentence and lost my ability to speak coherently. It took several attempts but I was finally able to swallow hard, the huge knot in my throat that competed with my attempt for any semblance of words, much less a full sentence. "Abel, me and your daddy have had such a hard time dealing with losing you and although we both know in our hearts that you are in Heaven, the loss, at times, is almost too great to bear." "Mommy talk to Jesus. He always helps me whenever I have a question or a problem." It was then that I felt the warmth of a gentle breeze and soft hand on my shoulder. I turned to look up into the face of Jesus and as I slowly stood to my feet, felt Him gently wipe a tear from my cheek. In His presence, I felt such warmth and love...almost as if

I were the only one in the universe. "Anna, my child, I love you. I have always loved you even before you were conceived, I knew and loved you. Come with Abel and Me for a visit as I have some people that have been waiting to see you."

It was then that we were standing within what appeared to be a city park, but a very large city park with sidewalks that bordered two sides of the park. Huge lush trees that were unlike any variety of tree I had ever seen, sat within the center of the park as well as each corner of the park and flowers of so many different kinds including; roses, lilies, iris, orchids, tulips, sunflowers, daffodils, hydrangea, amaryllis and so many more; some I did not even recognize. As I grew accustomed to my surroundings, I noticed people; people of all ages, different cultures, different races; all together. "Anna, I have someone here that has been wanting to see you." I looked up and saw my grandma. My grandma had died when I was 7 months pregnant with Abel and I had taken her death especially hard because we were so very close. She looked as she always did and yet different; a younger version of herself. Gone was the white hair, which now was replaced with a beautiful auburn color, dimpled cheeks and eyes of brown that twinkled when she smiled, especially when she laughed. "Oh grandma, I have so missed you!" "Anna come with me for awhile, and we can talk and catch up." And with that, she gently put her arm around my shoulder and gave me a hug and a nudge to start walking. "Abel, you don't have to let go of my hand; you can go with us." "I will take Abel with Me, but we will meet up with you later, I promise"...Jesus said.

As we continued our walk through the park, I noticed

that any individual that passed by always called me by my name. "Hello Anna, how are you?" How could they know me? How do they know my name? "Anna, I know that everyone has had a hard time with losing Abel, but especially you and Adam. Oh Anna, this Visit is a gift. A gift from your Father, God, because He loves you; He loves all of us and cares about every detail of our lives. Although in Heaven, there is no sadness, no grief, no pain, no tears, no anger, and no despair, we are still aware of these qualities that are present in our loved ones on earth. Do you know that I have watched you ache with the loss of your child, crying tears into your pillow masked by the silence and darkness of the night. Anna I am no longer of this earth, but you are and although I wish with every fiber of my very being and self that I could take this hurt, pain, anger and grief away from you, I cannot. Anna, God did not take Abel away from you. While we live on earth, we learn many lessons and have many unfortunate sometimes devastating situations happen but I promise you if you will only trust and know that God loves you, you will begin to heal."

I noticed as grandma was speaking a small little girl with long ringlets of red hair holding hands with a smaller little girl with a headful of blonde curly hair come up to us and "Mommy, who is this lady? She doesn't live in Heaven yet, does she?" It was then that grandma turned to me and introduced the two little girls..."Anna, this is Minnie Louise and her sister, Lilly; my daughters." "But grandma these two are yours? But how?" "Well you see when your granddaddy and I first married, we had a little girl and that was Lilly, the blonde haired one, but she died during the influenza outbreak of 1918." She was only 2 years old. We then had another girl, Minnie Louise. Minnie Louise was a good, robust healthy child but came down with a fever and chills and the country doctor prescribed medication, which she had a really bad reaction to and we lost her at the age of 6 years old. The medication had sulfa in it and back then I didn't know that really no one in our family can take sulfa drugs." I was shocked and as I stood there trying to regain my composure, remembered that grandma gave me my cue to respond to the introduction. "Well, hello Minnie Louise and Lilly, I am delighted to meet you." As if my grandma read my mind, she explained to the girls who in fact I was and that I was here for a short visit in Heaven. "Girls, Anna is Abel's mommy." "Girls, I will catch up with you, go ahead on the trail ahead of me." "Grandma, how did you manage after losing not one but two children and not completely lose all sense of reason?" "I did for awhile to be honest with you. I struggled for at least a year and even had the thought of taking my own life because I just couldn't bear the thought of living without both of my girls, but then I had the dream. God gave me the gift of a Visit from my girls in a dream one night. It was wonderful! I could see them, touch them, hug them and see that they were very happy where they were, which was such a gift, Anna! The dream was so real that I didn't want to leave or come back and actually woke with tears on my cheeks, but guess what I held in my hand? While in the dream, Jesus explained that I would know the Visit was very real because I would take something from the girls back with me and do you know what that was Anna? Each child in Heaven is given a golden ring from our Father. On earth we call it a baby ring, I had one, your mother had mine and you have your mother's. Both of my girls gave me their golden rings and when I awoke they were both in my hand."

"God knew that these rings given to me by my girls would help me in so many ways and he was so very right. Anna, these rings helped me remember even when I missed the girls the most and was feeling the saddest a soul can feel, that I had the promise of seeing them again and that they are loved and being taken care of by the Father. Because sin is so rampant within this world and bad tragic things do happen does not mean that God has allowed or caused this to happen. God does not cause bad situations or bad decisions but He can show you that He still loves you and does show each and every one of us daily. God gives each and every one of us free will and this very free will, caused sin within the world but God chose to pay the price for this sin and gave His only Son to pay the ultimate price. God did not take away our free will because he wants each and every one of us to come to Him by choice not because we have to but because we want to come to Him. What a gift and treasure this free will is that God has given to each of us. True love be it a father's love, mother's love, spouse's love or even a best friend's love is so much sweeter when it is given freely. Think of sweet Abel, as mischievous as he always was and still is, would you want to control his thoughts, attitudes, emotions, and behaviors, even the very people that he likes or loves? Well no, that is not love. Love is freedom, love is unselfish and love is kind." Grandma then slowly turned her head toward me and with a twinkle in her eye, winked and said "You know, that sounds like a Bible verse I know!"

"But grandma, the girls are still so little and they died so many years ago? Why have the girls not gotten older or aged?" "Time is irrelevant in Heaven, dear. Time exists on a continuum as in a straight or horizontal line and in Heaven we are given the privilege of having the choice of where on this continuum we choose to start or begin our journey. But remember, our "days" are not 24 hour days; one day can be the equivalent of 1000 years on earth. I know, I know, it's confusing and hard to fathom. I have chosen to "start" on my journey with my girls at the very age they were when they left me and watch and love them as they grow. See Anna, nothing is ever lost that our Father's grace and good will cannot reclaim for us, even the very sweet essence of time." As we continued walking within the park among the flowers, I welcomed the soothing quiet to reflect on all of the overwhelming information grandma had given me. Why had I tortured myself and worried about Abel when I knew deep down within the very fibers of my being, everything my mom had always taught me about God was true. Sure we buried Abel's body on earth but that body was not Abel, that body only held his spirit; his soul?

As the silence provided me with much needed focus and interpretation of all that I had learned within this Visit, it also provided me with the opportunity to really survey everything around us. It was bright as if the middle of the day, but there was no sun in the sky to be seen. Amazing as it sounds, each and every person in Heaven seemed to emit a glow; the glow seemed to project from the inside out. Each individual was "filled" with the glow but none in Heaven could compare to the glow of Jesus. In His presence; I felt warmth and love that flowed directly outward from His Being and it seemed to cover me like a warm, heated blanket from the cold. The joy I felt in His presence was indescribable. He possessed the purest and brightest glow that seemed to leap from His very fingertips. His intense glow did not strain or hurt my eyes; I felt the need to drink it in as much as possible. This glow seemed to light all four corners of Heaven. Seeing Jesus felt like coming home again with a striking familiarity that I just couldn't shake off. It was almost as if I had been here before, knew Him before, but how? When?

Almost as if cued by my thoughts to join us, I heard His voice, "Have you ladies gotten reacquainted yet?" With a ready smile, I spoke up, "Yes!" and clasped grandma's hand with both of mine. I felt like a giddy child again; happy in all of this knowledge I had been trusted with and in the joy of my reunion with grandma and Abel. Before I could reign my impulsive feeling in, I had already hugged Him (Jesus) in one full sweep with tears of joy and as I tried to pull back, He seemed to hug me all that much harder.

After a few brief moments, I pulled back and this time He did let me go but only to His arm's length and as He held my forearms and looked at me, I found myself saying, "Oh Father, thank you so very much!"

"You are quite welcome, my dear!" "Abel, I think we are going to the playground over there between the two trees and you can play with Minnie Louise and Lilly for awhile. Does that sound good to you Abel?" "It does grandma but I wanted to pick mommy some pretty flowers." "You can do that. We will make her a nice arrangement. I also thought we might try some of the orange and green fruits in the park. I've heard they are quite delicious!" And as grandma, Abel, Minnie Louise and Lilly walked away, they all turned in unison to wave, with grandma winking and blowing me a kiss and they were off to the playground. Jesus and I continued with our walk through the park quietly enjoying the interlude with occasional greetings to passerby's "Hi Amanda! How are you today?" "I'm wonderful! I love you Father!" I watched in awe, as He knew every single name of every individual and at times even stopped to give them a quick hug, throw a Frisbee, or even engage in a quick game of hop scotch or jump rope with the children, much to their delight! As we drew closer to the center of the park, I smelled the intense and sweet familiar smell of magnolia blooms and notice that the crowds have thinned with only a couple of individuals that pass us by with a ready smile and a nod. "Anna I know that you have questions for Me; please come over and sit awhile with Me on the bench." It's true, there are so many questions, but where do I begin?

"Anna, do you know what this place is?" "It's Heaven." "Yes you are right, it is. It is a place that I have prepared for those that love Me. When We formed man; he was formed in Our Image, greatly loved by Us, but formed with free will. Free will ensures that the love We receive is given freely and not forced. Forced love is not true love. There are many types of love; a spouse's love, a brother's love, a mother's love, a friend's love, and each of these different types of love are a gift. If you or any individual is forced to love his brother or sister, spouse or friend, would you take the extra steps needed to ensure that your spouse, loved one, family member or friend is safe, happy, healthy and free from any harm; the answer would be a probable no. Resentment becomes the burden that you must also bear with this forced love. We knew this when We created man and also knew that true, self-sacrificing, emotionally binding love comes when it is offered and given freely. But when given a choice; man, gifted with the free will, chose sin and since that time, sin has continued to manifest. With the manifestation of sin within the world; tragedy, suffering, illness, tribulation and even death do occur but they are a direct result of the sin introduced within the world. A result; they are not an action taken or a cause of; but a direct result!"

"The good news is I've paid the penalty for this sin and all future sin and do this from a place of love. The Father, Holy Spirit and I ask that you repent of your sins, have a relationship with Us daily through prayer, read the Word, and love Us with all of your heart, mind and soul. Each individual within the world ever born and yet to be born, We love completely. Abel is My gift to you as you were My gift to your mother and your mother was My gift to her mother and the list goes on and on. We knew when Abel was formed within your body that Abel's time on earth would not be for long; but his time in Heaven is infinite! I have heard the grumblings and the remarks from my children "Father, why do You take this one, when You should take that one, because that one is evil and wicked, but then only We can judge those individuals because We know the full measure of their life and their burdens they have borne. Could it be that We choose to take this one and not the evil one in hopes that the evil one will repent and be spared from eternal separation from Us? Yes that is the truth as We wish that all individuals live in this place called Heaven with Us, but then we come back to free will. Free will at times makes this improbable. Do you understand what I am trying to say to you?"

"I do!" And with that statement barely out, the dam ruptured and the tears came and would not stop! "I'm so sorry for all the anger and the harsh words that I've thought and said about You, Jesus! Please forgive me! Have I completely ruined my chances of going to Heaven when I die?" "No, my child you could never do that! Let me ask you this; was there ever anything that Abel could do or say that would make you love him any less?" "Well, no. While he was with me, he could really try my patience at times, but I could never, ever stop loving him!" "That is how it is with Us and you. There is nothing that you could do that would ever make Us stop loving you!" And with that statement, Jesus reached up with his fingers and wiped the streaming tears from my eyes and cupped my chin in his hand and gave me a wink and a smile!

We had just finished this exchange and had set down on a bench in the park, when I felt a tug and pull on my right sleeve and a tiny whisper in my ear behind a cupped hand; "I love you!" and I saw a little hand reach over and grasp my hand. Looking over to my right, I see a small child of about 3 or 4 standing there looking up at me with such love, such trust, and such warmth. This child has blonde hair, very light blue eyes, and freckles that sporadically dot her little nose and both of her cheeks and an odd familiarity about her that I can't quite put my finger on. This child is the very image of myself when I was younger with the only difference being that she's blonde and taller than I was at this age. "Well hello there, and who are you, my dear?"

"Anna this is Kathleen Ella and she has been anticipating this meeting with much excitement! In fact, it's all that we have heard about for the past little while!" And with that, Jesus winked at Kathleen Ella and laughed heartily out loud. Such an infectious laugh! "I love the name and was actually going to name my little girl, Kathleen Ella." "Well, I hope my little girl is as pretty as you are Miss Kathleen Ella! How old are you?" And with that question, Kathleen Ella held up her tiny little hand with only her thumb folded to show me that she was four years old. "I am 4 years old. I'm so excited to meet you. Abel told me that you were so pretty and so nice and such a good mommy!" Kathleen then walked over and climbed up on my lap and rested the back of her head on my chest.

"Anna, Kathleen Ella knows that Abel left his earthly body (and family) and came to Heaven to be with Me and his Heavenly family. Kathleen Ella is My promise to you of good things that still wait for you in this journey that you must continue and finish before you reach your final destination; Heaven. Kathleen Ella is the daughter of you and Adam and she will make her appearance in August of next year." I looked at Jesus, with my mouth wide open, staring at Him and then at her, then at her and then Him again, all the while the entire idea or notion not completely registering or working its way through my processors. "Kathleen Ella is my daughter? But how can that be? She has yet to be born on earth and yet here in Heaven she is already 4 years old?" "My child, I made the earth, I daily hang the clouds within the sky, thoughtfully placed and arranged each star within the night sky, and made the very first female from the rib of the very first man, can I not do this also? I have made the female body to grow, nourish and carry a child that begins with JUST one fertilized egg and develops into a fully developed baby within the womb that will be born and grow into adulthood, can I not do this also? All of the laws of the universe, I have set into place and everything under the sun is governed by these same laws but cannot the Lawmaker change these very laws that He has set into place? The answer is yes, I can!"

What a precious gift the Lord has given me! If only Adam could see her! She is absolutely perfect in every way and I know that my Adam would cherish her if only..."My child, why do you look so troubled?" "Jesus knowing that Kathleen Ella is coming to us is such a joy to me but we are not at a very good place right now. How do we get to where we need to be?? Adam won't talk to me and fills his days with work and alcohol to numb his pain. We barely talk now! We're only roommates and I don't see how that is going to change anytime soon." "Your loss of Abel is something that you and Adam will never completely heal from and you both will carry that loss with you but with time the sharpness of the knife of grief will lessen and the memories that you have, will sustain you. Although you both know in your hearts that Abel is with Me in Heaven, I know that you grieve because Abel is not with you in his physical body. Anna each individual grieves in their own unique and different way and although Adam's coping skills have at time been self-destructive, be patient with him, he will come around. His loss of Abel is no greater than yours , but is still very substantial and runs very deep within his very soul. I know at times, you have a hard time connecting and understanding Adam, but be patient, supportive, helpful and loving and you WILL breakthrough. It will happen, I promise you! Hold steadfast! Adam attempts to numb his sorrows with alcohol and work but those sorrows will have to be dealt with as they can only be pushed and held down but for so long. They will re-surface again and again and any attempts to assuage those sorrows will only increase the intensity of those feelings."

"Mommy, I am so excited to meet you! And I look a lot like my Mommy don't I?" With that question, Kathleen Ella turned to Jesus and Jesus nodded his head, smiled and with a rub of her cheek, He said "Yes you do, my girl!" "Mommy did you know that I picked you all by myself?" I saw how sad you are and thought I could make you happy!?" I just sat there staring; drink-ing in all of this wonderful elixir given to me by God, ready at any certain moment to erupt and overflow and completely consume my entire being with my love for this child; our child. "Do you and Abel spend a lot of time together playing?" "Uh huh, sure do and we have so much fun! We love to play chase, hide and go seek, and even play on the monkey bars! Abel says I hug him too much but I don't think I really do!" As she sat there talking to the two of us, I watched Jesus face as he lis-tened, totally enthralled with Kathleen Ella and with this comment he lets out a huge bellow of a laugh and grabs Kathleen Ella and hugs her to Him. "Sweet child, I will take all of the hugs that Abel chooses not to, how does that sound to you?!" "Good to me!"

"Persevere Anna in this; your time of trials and tribulation and take comfort in the Book that provides all of the tools that you want and very much need to get through this earthly life; the Bible. Psalm 46: 1-3 states "*God is our refuge and strength, a ever- present help in trouble. Therefore we will not fear, though the earth give away, and the mountains fall into the heart of the sea; though its waters roar and foam and the mountains quake with their surging.*" "If it were not so, I would not say it nor allow it to be written in My Book. Trials, tribulations, losses, tragedies, and misfortune do occur every day in this sinful world but as with a diamond that begins it journey within a rock in a mountain top; sanded and polished to perfection but still subjected to extreme pressures to accomplish the ultimate perfection; such are all of those that have endured trials and tribulations. For those that would pray to be humble and to understand those that live in poverty, would I not allow a season of poverty within their own lives? For those that would pray for the ability to not lose their temper and to have patience, would I not allow a season of testing to ensure that patience is learned and acquired?"

"Oh Jesus, I've been so mad at You for so long now and I'm so sorry!!" I couldn't even finish what I wanted to say as the huge lump in my throat threatened to steal my very words away! "Can you ever....for.. give me?" "Oh my child, of course I forgive you, I forgave you even before you asked! My love for you and Adam is immeasurable and like the "*Prodigal Son*" Adam will find his way back home and I will be waiting. Each child of Mine is very different in so many ways and yet each is very much the same. Some begin with a good foundation, their knowledge of Me and the Book of Love (Bible) building a sturdy foundation that will hold them together when they suffer through the harsh weathers of life. They in turn will look back and remember what they have been taught, seek solace in the Scriptures and seek Me. While others do not begin with a good foundation that will enable them to suffer through the harsh weathers of life and then turn to earthly things such as alcohol, drugs and sex for instant gratification. But it is then that I send them that someone with the good foundation that understands that it is only I that can calm the storms of life and that someone, works with them to help lay the foundation based on My Word and it is there that life begins anew."

"David's story in the Bible was always one of my mother's favorites. She would always tell me the story of David and Goliath, the giant and David's defeat of the great giant. David weathered many great storms within his life too, right?" "Ah yes, David, I love David and I know that he loves Me. David was so human in every aspect and yet his very soul held a piece of the Divine and do you know why?" "No, I don't; I know that David committed adultery with Bathsheba and had her husband killed in battle, but that is all I know?" "You are right, but David sought Me each and every time he made a mistake or sinned against Me, with a broken and contrite heart. The Lord looks directly at the heart of each individual and David's heart was pure love for Me. David was not perfect as none of My children are but he sought My counsel, My forgiveness when he sinned and he sought constant fellowship with Me. The Lord is merciful to those that appeal to Him with a broken heart; a broken heart moves the very heart of Me."

"Anna I have one more person for you to meet and then we can go catch up with Abel." "Okay that sounds good but I don't think my heart can take another wonderful surprise!!" As I said this, I could feel my anticipation almost begin to take my very breath away! "Kathleen Ella, would you like to continue with us on our stroll or go play on the playground?" "Can I play on the playground for a little bit?" "Of course you can!" And with that Kathleen Ella grabbed Jesus by the legs and hugged them tightly and He bent over and gently kissed the crown of her head. "Mommy, can I give you a kiss and a hug?" "Of course, my sweet!" As I squatted down on my knees to hug Kathleen Ella and she kissed my cheek, I almost felt the urge to hold onto her and never let go. "Mommy that's a good tight hug and look Jesus she's smiling but she has tears running down her cheeks, why is that?" "She's just very happy, those are happy tears; the very best kind of tears!"

Kathleen Ella skipped off to the playground singing with joy in her every step! Could I be any happier at this moment? I didn't think that was possible! We were going to have a little girl, a wonderful, perfect little girl!! As we continued our walk, I looked over at Jesus and really had a moment to study Him. His very Being glowed especially His face and He projected outward rays of pure warmth and love. It felt like the sun bursting through the clouds on a windy day, you could feel the warmth; it was almost tangible. He was wearing a long white robe with a golden sash at the waist but the robe, I'm sure was not made of earthly material as it seemed to glow also and was the softest yet the brightest white material I had ever seen; almost translucent. His skin was dark and He had a prominent nose with a full short beard that covered the lower part of His face. He had shoulder length hair that was the color of golden chestnut brown, but it was the eyes that held my attention. His eyes were a mixture of light blue and green. His eyes were warm, loving and caring and seemed to look right into my very being. I could see in His eyes the very reason for my being; His love....

As I was caught up in my thoughts, I heard "Yay, here they come!" And as I looked over at the park bench on the opposite side of the park, I saw a little boy of about 3-4 years holding a handful of balloons jumping up and down. He started running toward us and it was then that I noticed the dog running behind him. It couldn't be!? Could it? I had a dog growing up named Duke; he was an English Bull Dog and when he died our entire family took his death hard, especially my dad. Duke was solid white but had a round circle of color around his left eye and he was such a loving dog; he was part of our family. Almost as if hearing my thoughts Jesus said "Do you remember Duke?" "I do, I do! Animals can go to Heaven too?" "Of course they can. All animals great and small reside here in Heaven. They are a part of Our creation and We want them here for you to enjoy." As I leaned over to pet Duke, he raised his right paw to shake. I shook his paw and as I squatted down to talk with Duke, he jumped up on me and knocked me down, wagging his tail and barking....Duke remembered me!! My mom never allowed animals in the house, but with Duke she made an exception...I think he always knew he was the favorite of all of our animals! "It's so good to see you boy! I have missed you so much! I gave him a tight squeeze and kiss on the top of his head and a soft pat and turned my attention to my other visitor.

"And who are you with all these big, wonderful balloons that you have here?" "My name is Noah. Do you want a balloon?" "Why yes I think I'll take one!" "Anna, this is Noah and he is your little boy." "My little boy!?"

He had a headful of black curly hair (like me), deep choc-olate brown eyes (like Abel) and dimpled ruddy cheeks. "Noah, do you know who this is?" "This is my mommy and I love her!" With that being said, Noah stuck his little index finger in his mouth and gave both of us a half grin as if he had embarrassed himself. "Jesus told me mommy that I look like my daddy. Is my daddy with you? "No he is not with me right now. I'm sorry; I'm sure that he would very much like to meet you though." "Anna, Noah will come 2 years after Kathleen Ella and he will complete your family." "Mommy have you met Kathleen Ella? Me and her and Abel play together a lot! But she kisses us too, too much! Yucky!" With that be-ing said, we both break out in a fit of laughter as Jesus says "Poor Noah and Abel, you two have to put up with kisses from your sweet sister!" Noah then seeing me and Jesus laugh, starts laughing too and mimicking Jesus by placing his hand over his stomach while he is laughing. Such a sweet sight to behold! Jesus reached down and picked Noah up and gave him a kiss on the cheek and hugged him to Himself tightly and said "I love you very much Noah. You are a delight."

"Well look whose walking up to meet us!" As I turned to look over my right shoulder, I could see Abel, Kathleen Ella, and grandma walking together toward us. As my eyes made contact with Kathleen Ella and Abel, they immediately started running toward us as if seeing who could beat the other. Abel came up first in front of me and grabbed my hand and pressed it to his cheek. "Mommy I have missed you and daddy but Jesus promised that you will come and live here when it is time for you to leave like I did." "What do you have here?" "I picked some flowers for you, don't they smell so good?" And Abel handed me his bunch of flowers with blue, red, maroon, violet and yellow blooms. "Abel these are so beautiful! Did you pick these in the park?" "I did! I thought the flowers might make you feel better! Mommy don't be sad when you think of me. I am still here (pointing at my heart); I just have a different address now. Jesus makes the best promises! He promises that one day, you, daddy, Kathleen Ella, Noah, grammie and me will all live together here in Heaven and guess what? Here in Heaven we get to design our very own house!!" And with that Kathleen Ella yelled "I want stairs!" "Yeah me too" said Noah!

"Anna you still have so much to do on earth and it is time for you to go back now." "Jesus I have a question; will Kathleen Ella or Noah remember any of this visit?" "No, their memory will not retain any of this. New memories will begin with their physical birth." Grandma stepped forward and hugged my neck and as she drew back cupped my cheek in her hand and with a soft, barely perceptible whisper said "I love you so much, Anna." As I gave her a kiss and hugged her once again, I could feel the aching already with missing all of them! "I love you too grandma!" "Come over here my three little ones and give your mommy a great big hug!" And with that they came bounding over and jumped to hug me only to knock me over backwards in the grass. What complete joy I felt! I sat down on the grass and looked up at all three of them and caught Abel's eye and saw his right fist closed tightly as he handed me something. "Mommy this is for you. Whenever you feel sad or you're missing me really bad hold this and know that I am with Jesus!" I cupped my hand under his and felt something fall into my hand and as I looked

I remembered what grandma had told me about her story. There in my hand sat a little gold ring! I clasped it tight and held it up to my heart, trying to speak but the words would not come. They were stuck behind the huge lump in my throat!! Abel pulled his left arm from behind his back and handed me another collection of flowers even more beautiful (if possible) than the first; bright bold and beautiful reds, periwinkles, lavenders, pearl whites, and deep rich maroons. I just grabbed Abel and hugged him to me while I cried the tears that I had been holding back for so very long. "Thank you Abel, I will cherish this ring and these flowers from you....."

As I stood up to stare at my group of loved ones, I tried to memorize every little detail about them. Kathleen Ella, with her sweet, happy smile and beautiful crystal clear sky blue eyes that readily displayed complete and total trust, Noah with his sweet but mischievous smile and slight gap between his two front teeth and those beautiful big chocolate brown eyes! But I focused on Abel with a special intensity, gone in this instant is the mischievous little boy (that I last knew) and he is now replaced with a more mature little boy with a happy, serene smile that signifies true peace, happiness and contentment. My little boy's body may be buried on earth but his very essence; his true spirit was here with me now. I guess I always knew about Heaven, but I was worried that "the accident"; the drowning had taken all the sum parts of my child including his spirit....how wrong was I? But as I stand here and look at him, I know that this is Abel; this is the most important part of Abel....his soul, his true essence. I then almost started with the realization that my child is with his true Father and is now safe and happy! What more could a mother ask for? My life in the "real world" could never be the same now; I mean how could it, right? Abel has developed the gift of empathy; gone was the little boy that sought to get into any mischief at whatever cost or punishment it caused. In its stead, was a little boy that now had empathy and it was felt with the words that he spoke; his words of reassurance to me and his wonderful gentle hugs.

"But the fruit of the Spirit is love, joy, peace, forbearance, kindness, goodness, faithfulness, gentleness, and self-control.. as told by Paul in his Letter to the Galatians. Abel will manifest these fruits as he continues to grow spiritually in Heaven. Since Abel's arrival here in Heaven, his focus has been entirely on you and his father. As you can see, Abel is happy here but with his happiness also comes concern for you and his father. Heaven is a joyful place where there is no pain, sadness, hurt, anger, jealousy, envy; these are fruits of the sinful world. Abel knows that he will be reunited with you and his father one day and this brings him great comfort but he also want you to KNOW this. Know this truth without any doubt!" "I do Father, now I do know this with complete certainty! I know that Abel is well and this (as I cupped Abel's chin in my hand) is the essence of Abel, not his earthly body! Thank you Father! It was then that Jesus gave me a tight hug and told me "I love you my child, always! Never forget this! Do not let the world with its material possessions and uselessness grab onto your soul and hold it hostage, the real treasure is found within here, your heart!" as Jesus pointed to my heart with a wink and an easy smile.

As I slowly opened my eyes with my arms

outstretched in front of me, I realize I am sitting now on the side of my bed enclosed in the darkness of my bedroom with a singular glow of moonbeam stretched across my bed. My hands are clasped together holding the flowers tightly and as I open them I can see the ring in the palm of my hand! This was not a dream, not a dream at all!! My cheeks feel sore, I'm sure from the constant smiling and laughter that were fixed upon my face during my visit to Heaven. I again clasp the ring within the palm of my right hand and hold it up to my chest...."Oh Father, thank you so much!! This meant so much to me, more than You could ever, ever know!" It was then that the cascade of tears started falling, covering the tops of my legs as I look down and remember the joy of the Visit, my loved ones faces, and Abel. As I look over at the clock dial, it reads 3:00 a.m. Wow! A lifetime in only 30 minutes; grandma was right, time is different in Heaven. I ponder this as I go to the kitchen and grab a vase and fill it with water and place my flowers on the nightstand. These flowers are absolutely exquisite and look as if they have just been picked from a flower garden; and my only hope is that they will last a lifetime.....

Sleep evades me...Of course the sandman cannot be found! I endlessly toss and turn and finally look over at the clock...Its 4:27 a.m. Really? So I sit up at the side of the bed holding the ring, cherishing it, remembering my little boy as I kiss the ring and place it in my jewelry cove. I know I have a Bible but where is it? I'm ashamed to admit to myself; I don't know when I last opened my Bible....As I wonder through the house, it's so quiet; peaceful, serene and a perfect time for me to open and read the Word. Adam sleeps in the study and as I tiptoe through the dark study, my little toe snags on the corner of the coffee table and I cry out before I can catch myself! Adam sits straight up...."Is that you Anna?" "Yes, I'm sorry, I was looking for a book?" "Anna, you know that I have to be up at 6:00 a.m.!" "How am I supposed to sleep with you traipsing through the house during the night?" And with that he turned on the lamp.

I sat down on the end of the couch and nervously tried to approach the subject with Adam...."Adam, we need to talk; I've had an experience and I need to tell you about it! It's about Abel." I then attempted to tell him the story of my visitations but unsuccessfully as Adam angrily kept interrupting me...."Anna, have you been drinking!? Do you really expect me to believe this nonsense? Come on Anna! I am not a fool!! "But Adam, it's true, I promise..." "No, I don't want to hear about it!" But Adam, I have the ring in our room..." "Anna, you need help....Our boy is gone, leave me alone! You are delusional!!" Resigned, I became quiet and went over to the bookshelves and found my Bible and went silently out of the study with Adam mumbling under his breath as I walked out of the study....

Before I open my Bible, I say a small prayer of gratitude and open the Book of Matthew and begin reading. It is only when I hear Adam close the front door and leave that I realize that I have been reading nonstop for about 2 hours. I want to start my read with the Books of Matthew, Mark, Luke and John to better understand Jesus, who He is, His teachings, and His great love for us. How wonderful this Son of God is and how much He loves us.....

Even as I shower to get ready for my day, I am so lost

in my thoughts as I dry off with my towel that I almost don't hear the phone ring. "Hello." "Is this the Morese residence?" "Yes it is? May I ask whose calling?" "Mrs. Morese, this is the highway patrol and we're calling to inform you that your husband, Mr. Morese has been in an automobile accident and is now being transported to Saint Ava Hospital." "What!!? Is he alright? How did it happen??" "Mrs. Morese, do you have someone that you can call to drive you to the hospital? If you don't, we can send someone to drive you to the hospital?" "I can call my mother. Thank you." As I hang up the phone, panicked and breathing in short sporadic breaths, "Oh my God, no not Adam....not again.....! Oh God, please no!!!!

As we speed into the hospital parking lot, we notice two highway patrol cars with lights flashing, parked in the emergency room parking lot entrance bay area and I barely give my mom enough time to stop before I sprint toward the emergency room entrance...."Anna, be careful, you are going to hurt yourself. I hadn't even come to a complete stop before you jumped out of the car!" "Come on mom, let's go!"

As I burst through the emergency room doors, I'm sure I looked every bit the wild woman, but I didn't care a bit. I went up to the first young girl I saw at the nurses' station "Adam Morese? Do you know where they've taken him?" "He's in Bay 12, ma'am and you are?" "I'm his wife!" I go to grab my mother's hand and the young nurse stops me and matter of factly states "Mrs. Morese, we can only allow one visitor at a time, right now." "Mom, can you sit in the waiting room and I'll be back shortly. I have to go and check on Adam." As I go to head toward Bay 12, a highway patrolmen steps in front of me to block my path and with an apologetic smile extends his hand and says "Mrs. Morese, my name is Sergeant Hent and I need to speak with you for a moment." "But I need to check on my husband!" "I promise, it will only take a moment." "Okay." "Can you step into this room, please?" And with that he escorted me into an empty patient's room and closed the door.

I tried to appear calm but I felt like my insides were jelly, shaking uncontrollably! Can he see me shaking? I feel like I need to sit on my hands to hide their shaking...."Mrs. Morese, your husband, is intoxicated; he refused a breathalyzer at the scene of the accident but a blood test has been performed and it shows his alcohol level @ 0.12%." "What!!! He's drunk!?? Was he the only person involved in the accident? No one else?" I could literally feel the color draining from my face as I searched his face for an answer. "No ma'am, there was no else involved in the accident. This is very serious though!" "I know, I know!" "He will be charged for this; but there are some options that will be open for him and that will help him ultimately two fold. First, seeking treatment for this addiction in a treatment house and following through with this treatment until finished. First and foremost this will help him overcome his addiction, and secondly it will ultimately help him whenever he appears for his court session before the judge. Do you understand what I am saying here?" "Yes I do, officer. And thank you, I will speak with him about this!" And with that said, Officer Hent escorted me into Bay 12 of the emergency room.

As I walk into the Bay, my eyes are focused; searching intensely for Adam in the dimly lit area. As I lock eyes with Adam, because I know this man so very well, I can see almost as if for the first time; all the hurt, the heartache, the self-loathing Adam is feeling and my heart threatens to shatter into a million pieces. Barely perceptible to someone else, but I see it, if only for an instant or a flash of time, Adam's all consuming hurt but then it disappears as if it never were there at all. Adam bursts into laughter as he slurs his words...."Hey baby doll, can you believe that Officer Hent is trying to destroy all my fun? It's nothing serious....Look, look, I was looking down at my phone and going around a curve at the same time and, and skinned a tree. I didn't skin a buck, I skinned a tree...that was in the way, anyway!" With that, Adam puts his hand to his mouth and fakes serious concern..."Can you believe that? I was trying to help get rid of that damn tree, just trying to help them out and now they want to arrest me? Why are you looking at me like that, Anna? Don't you believe me?" Adam starts laughing; deep guttural laughing...and with tears from laughing, holding his stomach, he looks up at me and the switch turns off, so quick that I catch my breath because the room is now cold and hard. "You wouldn't understand anyway! You don't care about me....go ahead and tell the truth. Tell everyone, no wait I will"....and with that he shouts at the top of his lungs..."My wife and I are roommates, right baby? We just EXIST together....no cuddling, no hugs, no loving, just roommates!!" "Adam, now is not the time for this, listen to me." And I stooped down to eye level with Adam, grabbed his hands and pleadingly searched his face, the worn, worried, etched lines around his eyes....for any semblance of the man, that I fell in love with all those years ago. "Adam, Officer Hent is here because you were drinking and driving. Adam, I know that the man I fell in love with, is in there. He may be buried deep, but I know that he is trying to surface, trying to get his head above water....Adam, I know he's in there!" Our eyes locked and I felt the pain, the hurt and I understood. The understanding washed over me like a flood and I realized in that moment, all of the hurt and anguish that my husband, the man I had committed my life and very being to, had been carrying, barely able to function himself and yet everyday he carried this hurt and anguish, unable to help himself, even live life fully because of the tremendous weight of these burdens and I cried for my husband on that hospital floor. I cried for the man, who picked up these burdens, this man who sought to destroy himself but for the love and loss of his child.

Almost as if cued, I could see Adam softening, I could see the vulnerable side of my husband that he sought to clothe with alcohol, too much alcohol. Alcohol that was destroying his body, his mind, his inner peace and our marriage and I felt such a tremendous surge of loyalty, devotion and absolute love for this man. "Adam, you could have seriously injured yourself or someone else. Can you not see this? Adam, I need you to understand me. This is a turning point, a bend in the road, a new direction for both of us and I need you to listen to Officer Hent and what he has to say. Adam I am begging you...just listen." I had barely gotten the words out and Officer Hent, was at my side, his face partly hidden in shadows but the tone of his voice, well relayed the seriousness of the situation. Officer Hent sat down in one of the armchairs and explained to Adam, his options and what exactly he was up against. To Adam's credit, Adam listened, albeit even though I knew that if I could smell the alcohol on his breath and person, the officer surely could to, but he listened and I prayed in that instant that Adam would take to heart every single word spoken by the officer. He explained to Adam that he would go to jail that night but that I would be able to bail him out in the morning. The officer was stern; forceful in his mannerisms and speech but I could almost detect a subtle hint of sympathy, empathy in his words, especially when I interjected to explain that this had culminated because of the loss of our son. It doesn't matter, the circumstances, the hard lessons, the mistakes made, if you are a parent, you just understand. You understand because you cannot see or fathom yourself in that individual's shoes....having to bear the burden of the loss of a child. Parents should never, ever have to bury a child and no parent would never, ever want to be a member of this club....this club that Adam and I were exclusive members of....!

As I stood up to walk away and stand in the corner, while Officer Hent spoke with Adam, I felt my heart would surely burst when I heard my husband say to all of us in the room, "I am so sorry. I have let myself go down this dark road, this dark road by myself and I need help. I need help because I do not think I can do this by myself. Alcohol covers the hurt, alcohol numbs the pain! The pain that starts as soon as I open my eyes and even well into the night, when my son visits me in my dreams." Adam started to sob, not just a sob but a deep guttural sob that sounded like a wounded animal, a wounded human. "Can you recommend treatment, a facility that will help me with this?" And with that, Officer Hent advised Adam on treatment options that would benefit him long term as well as us (as a couple)...

Mom and I left, with her driving, there were no words spoken. There was none needed. I knew we had work ahead of us, but grandma had always told me that a double bound rope is always stronger than a single bound rope and it was in this moment, this moment of time, that I knew exactly what she meant when she said this! I can hear her words, her voice..."The couple that are pulling at each end of the rope represent a single bound rope. This single bound rope is useless, it's not strong, and will eventually break! Now with two people (a couple) working together, pulling together.... well they represent the double bound rope and any hurdles, troubles that may come their way...well, they don't stand a chance because this double bound rope will hold...it won't unravel and it surely will not break!" As I reflected on her words, words of truth, I knew, especially since Abel's death, that I had been pulling on one end of the rope while Adam pulled on his end of the rope. We could win this battle, this war for Adam's very soul. We could do this, but we had to do it together, we had to pull together, in the same direction. Mom dropped me off at my house, only to assure me that she was only a phone call and a few short minutes away. As I walked into our house, the house now had an odd energy. It didn't feel like home, just a building with no memories, no good times shared together, no hope of redemption. It was then that I went into my bedroom and sat on my bed and cried and cried. I cried so much and so hard that my head began to hurt. As I fell back on the bed and looked up at the ceiling, I cried to Jesus, to God. "Oh please, please, help us with this!

Help Adam with this battle; this fight."

I heard a siren go by the house and I sat up at the side of bed and looked at the clock. It was 8:30 a.m. and other than the siren going by, there was absolute stillness in the house. I then dropped to my knees, folding my hands as my grandma and mom had taught and prayed. This prayer was not a formal prayer, this prayer was spoken with a mixture of salt, tears, old wounds and words. This prayer to Jesus was intimate, personal, searching for a Father's comfort, a Father's understanding and it felt right. It felt good to release so many concerns, fears, worries…it felt good to speak my truth, knowing that the Divine and me were together, I felt my heart soar. I felt peace, the kind of peace that washes over you, the peace that doesn't come from any outward sources; no this peace came from the inside; this peace trumped all of my worries, this peace spoke softly to my soul and exclaimed…"It will be alright. Adam will be okay. I am in control, I have this. I'm your Father and I hear your prayers, I feel your hurt, I understand your tears; your fears. Every single one!" As I released all of this to Jesus (God), I realized in that instant, the true definition of prayer; intimate fellowship with The One that loves me the best and I sat in awe at the power of prayer, the magnificence of prayer! I was in conversation, on my knees with my head in my hands with the One that created me. The One that knew me, understood me; the One that truly understands unconditional love. As I finished my prayer, I lowered my head in total submission, total relinquishment of all my fears, concerns and worries and I focused solely on Him; and my relationship with Him. I knew that the road we were currently on is treacherous, with grenades planted at every turn; waiting to catch us, unaware and to destroy us. These grenades (fruits of the world) are called by several names....hurt, rage, self-loathing, pride, and bitterness but then I know that these very same grenades have absolutely no power or control over the One that can quell life's forces ; the One that can calm the raging storm, the One that can still the turbulent waters. That day, I left that huge all-consuming bag of burdens, worries, concerns, and helplessness at the Master's feet. Oh I tried to pick that bag up again several times; only to feel Jesus pat my hand and say; "Give those to Me, I can handle that bag, the bag is light for Me." Such love, love manifested in Human/Spirit/and of God.....this love, I've never known, this love is absolute, true and perfect.

A lovely lady by the name of Ludie, called me, two to three times weekly, specifically during those first 2 weeks to inform me of Adam's progress, his treatment and his mental state. She worked in conjunction with several team members including; Thomas, Landis and Paul and I was so grateful for each and every one of them. Adam, Ludie informed me, had given the okay for me to be kept abreast of his condition; his missteps, his improvements, his treatments, his moments of understanding and clarity but in the area of counseling; Adam asked that this part of his treatment be confidential and I understood this. Oh how I longed to hear of the counseling sessions, but I understood (and still do) that this part of his recovery was sacred and personal. Ludie explained that this part of his treatments was THE most important; this part of his treatment, determined the very heart of the matter, the reason for his self-destruction. This part of the treatment explained everything; his reasoning, his actions, and his subsequent reactions and feelings of helplessness. Adam was never one to speak in depth about his feelings and when he did open up, it was only with close family members and friends; so I knew that this part of his treatment would or could be quite difficult for him. In his 3rd week of treatment, I received a call from Ludie to advise that the physicians felt it imperative to increase his counseling sessions to four times within a weekly period. When I asked about his physical state, I could hear the apprehension and trepidation in her voice when she informed me that the physicians were monitoring his vital signs closely; specifically his blood pressure, which had increased significantly during treatment. I asked her about medications and she provided a couple that were helping stabilize his blood pressure (in addition to other medications the physician ordered); Labelotol and Clonidine. I continued with my daily prayers, as they provided such comfort during this storm; this siege that Adam and me were under.

As I sit here at the window sill of one of our favorite local restaurants; and look outside the window, at the fiery red leaves, the golden, bright shiny leaves and even the rich, dirt brown colored leaves all swept up together in a Fall dance, buoyed by the tremendous, sometimes breath catching winds of Fall, I am reminded of the majesty of just these moments; these still quiet moments of wonder, watching Mother Nature as she performs her very last dance, before she settles in for a long winter's nap. The Golden Ring of Abel's rests on the juncture of the knuckle of my middle finger and as I look at it, I say a prayer of gratitude and thanks for this Gift; this treasure. And so the story goes... that the middle finger is directly related to the heart, the middle finger has veins, arteries, capillaries that traverse directly to the very heart of every individual and it is here that I will keep my Golden Ring, my treasure of my Abel; a remembrance of him, his life. This second finger with my Golden Ring also serves to remind me, as it is the second finger on my hand, that I am second. I am second in all things; that before I hurt with my words or action, I consider my actions, my reactions, my words, even my thoughts. The Holy Trinity is the first finger of my hand; it is bare, no jewelry; no decoration because the Holy Trinity and I will have nothing that stands between us.....nothing man-made, nothing of this world....I have a direct link through Jesus, my Savior...as we all do! I will remember this...always, never to forget that I am but second in all things, with Christ as the First, my Authority, my Father. I hear a swoosh and feel a wind and as I look up, I see mom setting her bag down with her purse at her leg side and her exclaim; "Penny for those wonderful thoughts, Anna? Your face is glowing my beautiful girl! Love you, I'm so sorry I'm running behind....my absolute pet peeve is to follow behind someone that brake checks constantly!" I laugh as I look up at her settling into her chair....., "Mom, they may be reminding you that you could possibly be too close. No one wants an uninvited visitor in their back seat!" And we both laugh at that absurd idea, but me knowing all too well that this woman, does indeed ride other cars way too close for comfort. "Hush, hush now and tell me what's going on with you?"

And we settle in for a nice meal, fellowship, laughter and love. Mom orders the baked fish, with a side of green beans cooked with almonds, and a large order of apple tots, with a nice side salad. I opted for the blackened fish covered with a light almond and lemon sauce, an order of the famous hush puppies and a large order of slaw. When we had finished, I looked at my watch..."Mom can you believe it's already 3:30? Where has the time gone?" She looked surprised..."Oh my gosh, time has surely flown by? I've missed my appointment with my hair dresser! "Let me call her and apologize! I've never, ever done that! Do you know it seems as if here lately, my memory has left me! Even with small things......one of the prices I guess you pay when you live a long time on this earth." "Mom I'm twenty four years younger than you and I have to write myself notes; and forget remembering all of my passwords. I bet I've changed my email password twice this month. I would guess that Adam and with everything that he is going through, my worries for him and how he's doing in his treatment, takes up a lot of my brain power!" You want to order a dessert, mom? Remember I'm treating today as you treated the last time." "You know, I think I will order something. Can you get the waitress attention?" I waved our waitress, Candice down and mom ordered her signature blueberry pie with maple nuts baked into the crust and I ordered the cherry pie topped with a small serving of vanilla bean ice cream. As we finished our desserts, we both set in silence, enjoying the moment. Candice, came back to our table, "Can I get you anything else? Oh come on, you've still got a little room in there!" "No, no, no Candice, no tempting, it's hard to turn you down. How's our favorite waitress doing today?" "Well, I'm doing absolutely wonderful, thank you for asking. I got a surprise last night when I got home" and Candice holds up her left hand with the most beautiful, most exquisite, Safire ring surrounded by three diamonds on each side. "He popped the question again last night and I took him up on it! He got on one knee and as he asked, he started crying. Well of course you know that upset our son (Lance) and he was like..."Mommy what's wrong with daddy?" I told him, "Daddy is happy, baby...those are tears of happiness!" Candice, had for as long as I can remember, waited on all of us. All of her customers loved her. She is always the same whenever we see her....beautiful, funny, loving, caring and always, always the advocate for those less fortunate. I can't count on my two hands, just how many times, that I've seen her go outside of the restaurant and invite someone in that couldn't afford a meal, feeding them I'm quite sure with her tips of the day or comforting one of her customers that needed some extra tender loving care. What an absolute jewel this sweet Candice is....I just know that her mom and dad are so proud of the young woman that she is, that she shows the world every single day. My phone started ringing with a tune from one of our local bands and Mom exclaimed..."I like that tune....quite catchy!" I smiled as I answered the phone..."Hello, yes this is Anna." "Anna, this is Ludie. Not to alarm you, but I need to talk with you. Are you by yourself or currently with someone?" "I'm here with my mom, enjoying a late lunch but it's all my mom's fault....she loves to talk as much as I do, but.."Anna, listen to me but I need you to remain calm, okay?" "Okay, what's up..... you don't sound like yourself, Ludie?" " Anna, can you meet me at the hospital? Adam, has had an event and is being transferred now to the hospital." "What!?

What's wrong, what's going on? Is Adam okay?" "The physicians that are taking care of Adam think that's he possibly had a stroke. We don't know any of the details yet but I need you to remain calm; for you and Adam's sake." My mom, then realized that this conversation was not a typical conversation; I guess the look in my eyes and the absolute fear in my face said it all. Mom then grabs my arm softly and interjects..."What's wrong Anna?" "Hold on mom, I'm talking with Ludie, hold on just a moment." "Which hospital Ludie, Saint Ava or Eastland Ridge?" "He is being transported to Eastland Ridge." "Okay, I'm on the way now!" "I'm on my way and I will meet you at the hospital, Anna." As I hung up the phone, my thoughts were racing back and forth, feelings of helplessness that were a constant after Abel's death, resurfaced and completely draped my entire being and somewhere in the midst of those racing thoughts, the apprehension, the shock, I looked down at the Golden Ring, the beautiful, exquisite Golden Ring on my second finger and I remembered. I remembered that Jesus is first and I am second. I remembered the Great Love and the Master of it all and I heard the small, still voice and felt His Great Presence...."It will be alright, Anna. I am here and I've always been here. I will never leave you!" "Mom, the physician's are thinking that Adam had a possible stroke and an ambulance is transporting him to Eastland Ridge right now." "Oh my, Anna!" This was all that my mom kept saying over and over..."Oh my, Anna!" Candice fortunately had heard the conversation and exchange and grabbed my mother's keys and said "I'm driving both of you! No quarrels, no arguments, let me do this!" We gladly relinquished this job to Candice, thankful that we had her with us. Candice went and explained the situation to her boss and met both of us at the side door and we went in my car to the hospital.

A normal drive to this hospital was 20 minutes from in town, but this ride felt like so much longer. Everything and everyone were in slow motion much as when you watch a replay of events and time seems to stop; stop in its very tracks. With the culmination of all my feelings, each fighting for supreme control of my thoughts, Mr. Time himself seemed to hold up his hand and exclaim..."This is too much for her, so I'm stopping for a short while, so she can catch up with us." But even with the entirety of my feelings; feelings of panic, worry, concern, and helplessness; peace, my new Friend came and comforted me. This Peace was assured, calm, still and quiet and this Peace has a name and His name is Jesus. This Peace hugged me and kept me warm, with feelings of calm, peace, assurance and an absolute knowing that everything would be alright.

Candice and mom dropped me off at the emergency room exit and went and parked the car. I ran in at full speed straight up to the counter..."I'm here, do you know where he is? We got here as fast as we could!" The older lady at the counter spoke in a monotone voice..."Who are you here for ma'am?" "My, my husband is Adam Morese and he should be here? He's had a stroke." "Ma'am he's in with the physician right now, but let me take you back to where he is. He's in emergency room #7. Come this way, please.""As we were walking towards the back and Adam's room, I felt a soft tap on my shoulder and looked over and stopped and saw Ludie standing there focused, serious..."Anna, do you need me to go with you?" "Yes, that would be wonderful, thank you!" She grabbed my hand and held it tightly as we walked down the short hall. As we circled around to the back row of rooms and the ER receptionist opened the door, I heard her softly say to the physician..."Dr. Bliven, this is Mr. Morese's wife here to see him." I looked to the physician for a sign of the seriousness of the situation, and even though his face remained neutral, his eyes gave away the severity of the situation. "Come in and sit down for a moment, Mrs. Morese and I'll explain Adam's current situation and help you with any questions, that you may have" and with that comment he motioned toward one of two chairs situated in the corner of the exam room. "Please call me Anna." Have you verified that it is indeed a stroke?" He glanced over toward Ludie and said softly "I have to ask you because of HIPAA laws, and privacy; can I speak freely about Adam's condition?""Yes, you can. This is Ludie,....she has been involved in Adam's care at the facility. She has been a wonderful, touchstone to me. She keeps me abreast of everything that is going on with Adam. I am so grateful for her!"I looked over at Ludie and squeezed her hand....sending a grateful look of appreciation! Dr. Bliven continued....."I'm sorry, we always have to ask to clarify....Adam has had something that we call a TIA, which can be a prelude to an actual stroke. Within the last day, the facility advised that his blood pressure has been highly elevated and even with the blood pressure medications that we have in place, we've seen his blood pressures spike to 220/115, and we've recorded four separate incidences of this at the facility. Right now his blood pressure is at 196/120. We are working with adding a couple of more medications in addition to the ones that he has been taking. These medications are given as needed, specifically when we see a spike in his blood pressures. I'm going to order that Adam be transferred to a room and that we keep him here a couple of days to monitor him. He has felt some weakness in his left arm, left leg and the left side of his face. We are going to watch him closely and we are hopeful that we can get a handle on Adam's spikes in blood pressures; it's imperative that we do this. Do you have any questions for me?" I didn't even pause to think as my questions tumbled out..."Do you or the other doctors think this is possible? You know that he is in alcohol withdrawal?" and even as I said this,Dr. Bliven started shaking his head...."Yes we do and that's why it is imperative that he stay here in the hospital and we monitor him closely for a few days. We gave him 4mg of Ativan to help him rest and he is sleeping right now. I am sure that shortly they will be transferring him to a floor but..., but".........and he paused for a moment as I heard over the hospital intercom..."Stroke Alert, Dr. Bliven please call extension 2004....Stroke alert, Dr. Bliven please call extension 2004." He then looked at me and gave me a reassuring pat on my arm, "Anna, I've got to go now, but I'll be rounding later on tonight. I am having him transferred to the ICU so we can better monitor his vital signs and condition. Please, if you have any questions or need to talk with me, let his nurse know and she will get in contact with me. Anna, we have medications that can help control Adam's blood pressure and I promise you that we will take good care of him." And with that he walked to the door and looked back as I said "Thank you Dr. Bliven."

My attention then turned directly to my husband,

focusing, watching him sleep, loving him. The sight of my husband, felt like refreshing rain on a hot steamy day, it felt like the first warm rays of sunshine that burst through the heavy trees after Mother Nature has decided to spread her blanket of snow for the little ones. Oh how I've missed him; missed seeing his face, being near him. It felt familiar, it felt like love, he felt like home to me. I pulled a chair up to the side of the bed, held his hand and bowed my head. "Oh Father, I come before You now, with a heart full of hope, a heart full of pain, begging please...heal him and make him whole. Convict his heart Lord and make it Your Own. I come to the Cross and give You this because I cannot carry it alone. Please Father, heal him, convict his heart and make him whole. I know that I am the worst of sinners, I fall short every day....every single minute of every single hour of every single day...but Father I would ask that You hear me, please hear me. Please forgive me for my sins; known and unknown. Thank you for Your unconditional love, thank You! I ask all of this in Jesus most precious Name.....a Name above all others. Thank you....thank you!" The river of tears shed at that bedside on that day...soaked the arm of my jacket and Adam and my hands that were held tightly together by an absolute love. As I finished praying, someone opened the door and said "Mrs. Morese, we are going to move your husband now up to his room." I looked up and saw his nurse coming toward me, and as I stood there for a moment, she touched my back and said "His nurse will be Jacqueline. She's wonderful and will take excellent care of your husband. I promise!" Two transporters appeared at the bedside, and as I gathered my things, the nurse stopped his IV fluids and placed him on a monitor. I heard a beep and the monitor started up with a display of heart rate and blood pressure. I asked her about the lines on the monitor and she stated "Those also monitor his heart rhythm as well as his other vital signs." She advised me of Adam's room number and I looked over at Ludie, who had been sitting quietly in one of the armchairs....."Thank you Ludie, you go home and be with your family....I'll keep in touch with you, I promise!" She held out her arms to offer up a hug and I gladly took her up on the invitation! "Thank you so much for being here with me. You are a Godsend!" And I went ahead to his room while they were preparing him for the journey via the elevator to his room.

After he was settled in and was resting, I closed my eyes, hoping this would shut my mind off and fortunately rest finally did come. I awoke to alarms and bells going off and someone nudging me on my shoulder...."Mrs. Morese, I'm going to need you to go to the waiting room.""What's going on? Why is everyone in here? Why is he shaking back and forth? Oh my God! What's happening!" With those last two comments, Jacqueline grabbed my arm softly and we went out into the hall. "Mrs. Morese, sorry, I mean Anna, it looks as if his blood pressure spiked again and we are working on lowering it." "Why was he shaking back and forth in the bed?" "We think that the high blood pressure coupled with the withdrawal from the alcohol has initiated a seizure, but listen, listen....we have some really good, smart doctors in there with him and I promise you as soon as he is stable, I will come and look for you and tell you everything that's going on. I promise!" I searched for a waiting room near to his room and found a corner, where I could collect my thoughts.

After what seemed a lifetime, I saw Jacqueline rounding the corner and walking towards me, with a physician behind her. "How is he doing? Have you been able to control his blood pressure? Has his seizures stopped?" As Jacqueline softly grabbed my hand, the physician pointed toward a group of chairs lining the back of the waiting room. "Mrs. Morese, I am one of the physicians taking care of Adam and we have gotten his blood pressure stable; we've given him medications to lower his blood pressures and calm his seizures, but, but there's more." "What is it? Tell me!" "Adam has suffered a stroke. It's affecting the left side of his body; his arm, his leg and there is some drooping with the left side of his face. We have scanned Adam's brain and there is no bleeding on the brain. This stroke was more than likely caused by a clot that broke off and traveled to the brain. I was looking at Adam's history and read that he has a history of high cholesterol and high blood pressure, Does he regularly see his doctor for the treatment of these?""Yes, although Adam has had his issues, he does see an internist, not as often as I would like, in fact, I think he had a appointment with the internist last week....no, maybe the week before? I know that he takes a medication for his blood pressure as well as his high cholesterol levels....I can't remember the names of his medications, but his physician prescribed them a couple of years ago." "Mrs. Morese, we think that Adam has not been taking his medications, and that fact coupled with his current withdrawal from alcohol, has proved only to aggravate his condition. "What? How can that be? How did I not know this?" "Mrs. Morese...." I interjected here with a "Please call me Anna." "Anna, with Adam's history also of alcohol abuse, we surmise that he has been on this self-induced path of destruction for awhile. I really do not want to get too personal here, so let me tread lightly" and then he paused for a long second and asked "I know that you and Adam lost a child within the past year or year and a half;...has he sought counseling for dealing with this loss." "No, not at all. He refused to attend our child's funeral and has not talked to me about how he's feeling. I mean, really talk to me. Other than when he's mad, angry or upset about something and then I can see his grief ooze or overflow to the top and only then does he dive into his alcohol to assuage and numb those feelings. And when his grief overflows, he doesn't react as I do....he's angry, I mean truly angry. Personally, I was hoping that with the counseling sessions within the rehabilitation facility, this might give him an outlet to pour out his anger, his bitterness, his grief, but now this has happened! Oh my God, what am I going to do?" "Well first of all, we gave medication for his stroke....if it is given within 3-4 hours of a stroke, this medication as well as Adam's body can begin healing itself, albeit still with possible long term rehabilitation. Adam is showing deficits from the stroke such as weakness to his left arm, his left leg and some weakness with the left facial muscles but we are hopeful for a positive outcome with this situation." It was then that I grabbed the physician and hugged him tightly! "Really you think so?" "I do!" As I straightened out the front of his coat, I apologized for the impulsive hug. "No worries, here. I understand. Now go in there and spend some time with your husband."

As I went into Adam's room, I watched him as I pulled up the recliner chair to the side of the bed. I was exhausted and sleep came readily as I would begin to doze off but would catch myself and sit up in the chair or stand up and walk around his room. I didn't want to sleep, I wanted to stand vigil by his bedside.... maybe some cold water on my face would help. I tried this and it did work for awhile. I reached into his bedside stand and pulled a Bible out that I had seen before while in the room. The Bible looked brand new, no pages turned down, no notes taken, I noted as I turned to the Book of Psalms. My grandma had always told me that a well used and read Bible leads to a happier, more focused life; a life with purpose and meaning. In addition to Psalms 46, my grandma loved Psalms 94 and as I turn to the page in the bedside Bible to Psalms 94, one verse (verse 19) seems to stand out; grab my attention, my focus..." *When anxiety was great within me, Your consolation brought me joy.*" Oh Lord, Your consolation; Your steadfastness, Your compassion and Your love.....brings me joy, focus, direction, an understanding...and an assurance that cannot be discarded; an assurance that brings me subtle but unquestionable seamless peace.

I find myself remembering happier times. Happier times when my Abel was so young; so little. It's a Sunday morning and I am trying to get Abel up and ready for church. Abel was, I think 4 at the time and I walk quietly into his room, give him a soft kiss on the cheek, nudge his shoulder and whisper..."Hey buddy, it's time to get up and get ready for church." Now anyone that knew Abel, absolutely knew that he was not a morning person, much like his mom. He opens his eyes; eyes that are open and awake but still groggy, vague and confused. "Mommy, I tired. I stay in the bed." "No Abel, sweetie it's time to get up! I've let you sleep a little bit longer because I know how much of a morning person you are not!" Abel then sits up in the bed, rubs his eyes and advises me...."Mommy can I wear my pajamas to church?" "Of course you can't! You need to wear your nice church clothes." "But mommy, Jesus don't care what I wear to church as long as I be there, right?" I laugh to myself as I savor this memory, this funny kid...."You are right, Jesus just wants us to be at church, but now silly boy, does mommy wear her pajamas when she goes to work, to church or out with you and daddy?" "No, but you know you could, mommy? Jesus won't mind at all!" That morning turned out to be quite difficult as I wanted Abel to wear his nice sweater and dress pants, but this little boy wanted to wear his camouflage jumpsuit with his bright orange hunting cap (that matched his daddy's). He was not happy at all but I did finally win that battle; granted, I knew how stubborn, how obstinate Abel could be and I celebrated this victory. Abel did wear his nice sweater and matching cache dress pants, but his displeasure was obvious to anyone and everyone that talked with him. As we were leaving out of the church vestibule, Ms. Sadie exclaimed..."Oh how handsome and nice you look, Abel!" I responded with...."Abel, can you tell Ms. Sadie thank you?" "Thank you, but Jesus don't mind that I wear my pajamas to church, does He?" "Well no He doesn't, not at all, but you sure look nice today, sweet Abel!" And by the time, we had gotten to our car, the snipped on tie was off as well as his jacket and thrown in the back seat of our car. He was a stubborn one, but he definitely got a good, full measure passed onto him from me, his grandma and his great grandma!

I can remember arguing with my mom too about wearing what I wanted to wear to school and I was not backing down either. I couldn't have been 6-7 years old and I was absolutely set on wearing a pull over sweater to school with a shirt underneath, but neither matched at all! As my memory serves, I argued and argued with my mom about wearing that mismatching shirt and sweater to school....until my grandma and granddaddy came over that night. Grandma was pure gold, she understood me, my frustration. "Baby, that is fine and well if you want to wear the shirt with the pull over sweater but you do know that when recess comes...you will be so hot! Your hot-natured anyway and now won't you be miserable and not be able to enjoy your day at school?" To me, a 6-7 year old, that made perfect sense and I relented, much to my mom's relief, not realizing that at any time during the day, I could have taken the ill-matched sweater off anyway! I just knew that my grandma made perfect sense to me!

As I was remembering and reminiscing, Dr. Bliven walked into Adam's room. "Anna, we've done some blood tests on Adam, specifically a test called a D-dimer, which when elevated can show or reflect a possible blood clot within the lungs and Adam's results are elevated. Now this doesn't positively mean that he has a blood clot, but I would also like to do another test called a duplex scan just to ensure that Adam does not have any abnormal clotting. It's noninvasive, but it's a good indicator and if he does have any clotting, we can start him on treatment right away." "If he does have clotting that shows, what treatment would you start him on?" "Well, because he was given medication; tPA, which is basically a blood thinner, at the first initial signs of his stroke, we will hold off for now with any further medications. Of course we will continue with his scheduled blood pressure medications and Valium as needed, but should his D-Dimer test be positive, we will still need to wait at least 24 hours before starting him on another medication for clotting." "Dr. Bliven, that sounds good to me, anything that will help him." "I'll go ahead and order the test and will advise you of his results." "Thank you Dr. Bliven!"

I grabbed Adam's call light and gently pushed the red button...."Can I help you?" "Yes, can you send the nurse into room 7A. I need to speak with her for a few minutes." "Yes ma'am. She'll be in shortly." Another 5 minutes had passed and Adam's room door opened and his nurse advised..."Mrs. Morese, did you need me?" "Yes, I am going to go home just for a couple of hours. Can you please call me on my cell phone if his condition changes while I'm gone." "Yes ma'am, let me verify your cell phone number while I'm in here." "My cell number is 206-555-0000.Thank you and thank you to all of the nurses....all of you have been so wonderful!" "Thank you, Mrs. Morese, I will let the other nurses know. Dr. Bliven has ordered another test for Mr. Morese and the transp.....well speak of the devil, here they are to transport him for his test." And when they had sent him on his way for the test ordered, I made my way out to my parked car and just set in the car, for a full 5-10 minutes before I cranked up the engine; just sitting in my car, enjoying the absolute tranquility of the moment.

I was able to enjoy, albeit even though restless, a full two hour nap at home, when my phone rang...."Hello." "Anna, this is Dr. Bliven, we've gotten the results of the scan and although Adam's test results were elevated, he doesn't have any clots, which is good news!" "But why was the blood test elevated?" "This could be for a number of reasons, but specifically it can just be contributed to everything that is currently going on within his body....the elevated blood pressure, the stroke and the resulting effects of the stroke on his body. It could be any of these things." "Thank you for calling me, I will be up there shortly to check on him."

I knew that Adam was in the best place possible for him right now. I can hear my stomach growling relentlessly and go into the kitchen and make me a bowl of tomato soup and a grilled cheese sandwich. Probably my dad's most favorite meal ever! He had to have emergency heart surgery when he was in his early sixties, and the hospital was strict.....cardiac diet, which basically meant little or no salt. As there were four of us totaled including; my sister and two brothers, each and every time any one of us went up to the hospital to see dad, he always smiled and winked and asked "Hey, can you get me a couple of extra salt packets?" I laugh as I remember this....because nobody would relent until dad urged one of us to try his "cardiac meal" at the hospital....I think my youngest brother did and the look on his face was absolutely priceless! "Anna, that food is so bland; so tasteless. I'm going to get dad a couple of salt packets down in the cafeteria.....maybe he can hide them and just use them when he needs some salt; because goodness, that food is the absolutely worst, and you know how dad is with the salt at his house." I could only nod and smile; dad rarely used the pepper but he salted all of his food to his taste! Dad was eventually discharged home and I swear it became an everyday

middle of the day meal for him! Grilled cheese with tomato soup......and we all know just how much salt really is in the tomato soup. We all talked with him about
his salt intake...and he would always quietly reassure
us that he was taking care of himself. "Listen, your dad
is no slow leak, I promise you! I am taking care of myself and my body; I don't ever, ever want to go through
that kind of surgery again. And besides, your ole dad
is tough; getting older but still tough, made from good
stock!"

The idea of a long, sweltering hot bath soak seemed
such a small, wonderful reprieve and as I undressed
and set down in the bath filled with lavender salts and
just a dash of Epsom salt, I completely cleared my
mind; focusing on the quiet, the stillness and it was
sheer heaven. Daphne, our Golden Retriever, stayed
close; curled in a ball at tub side, with an occasional
walk to the bath and resting her head on the side of the
tub. I think that she senses something is amiss. Right
after we lost Abel, amidst my drench; my flood of tears,
I could always look up through tear soaked eyes to see
her at my side, always close by to comfort me. I know
that she misses Abel. So many times, when I've looked
around the house for her, I find her in his bed or ly-
ing on his comforter. Does she sense that he won't be
coming back? Oh the wonderful times her and Abel
enjoyed together. As a small child, he often pretended
that Daphne was his horse and would ride her across
the prairie(our yard) as he searched for the bad guys.
Abel loved the idea of being a cowboy, with his beige
cowboy hat that completely covered his little ears; and
I in the kitchen would always chuckle as he came into
the "saloon" to get his fix of a cold glass of milk. He

would chug it down, wipe his arm across his mouth and say "Well, little lady....I got to get me some bad guys today!" As I checked on him outside the kitchen window, I could see him trying to ride his horse; Daphne, our Golden Retriever and could only chuckle at my little boy's imagination and watch poor Daphne as she did her best to accommodate him! What a wonderful, patient, loving fur baby she is! How lucky are we to have her.....

After getting dressed, feeding Daphne, and checking the mail, I pick up my small bag of essentials and head out for the hospital. Surprisingly traffic is light and I call mom to fill her in on the details...."Mom, I'm headed back to the hospital. Adam is in the Unit now, with his spikes in blood pressure and the stress that his body is under, Dr. Bliven told me that Adam has definitely had a stroke" and there was a long pause on the phone...."Mom, are you still there?" "Yes, I just can't believe it, Anna! He's so young.....how is he doing?" "Well, I talked with the doctor and he told me that because he's had a stroke, they only had about a 3 hour window of time to give him a medication to help prevent long term effects from the stroke and luckily they were able to give him the medication, within the window of time. So right now they are closely monitoring him. He does have some weakness to the left side of his body; his arm, his leg and some drooping to his face..." "Oh Anna, I am so, so sorry...what can I do to help you; anything?" "Well, mom I'd appreciate it if you would just check on Daphne for us and I've picked the mail up at our mail box but if you would pick up our mail at the post office box, that would be great!" "Sure no problem, no worries....I've got it handled. Anna, please, and as your mother, I'm saying this....please make sure you don't forget to eat! I know that you are just like me; when you're stressed, you don't want to eat and have no appetite, but you have to keep your strength up and I don't want you to get sick." "I promise mom, I'll remember to eat something! Thank you for doing that for us, I really appreciate it!"

As I walked off the elevators and onto the 7th floor, I was looking down at my phone and glanced up at the nurse's station to find all of the nurse's staring at me. When I looked up and saw this, all of them turned away, with a smile that didn't quite reach their eyes. Puzzled I went to the nurse's station and asked for Jacqueline. "She's in a room right now, but I'll send her to your husband's room when she's through. She's actually taking care of Adam today." I paused and looked at the nurse for a thoughtful moment, searching to find something in her demeanor, her stance, her fake smile....but she never betrayed her true feelings. I couldn't quite decipher her mood. Strange!? "Thank you!" As I walked away, that sixth sense, that feeling in your gut (that tells you something is not quite right) was piqued and on high alert, and I felt my throat go dry and felt myself unable to take a deep breath.....come on Anna, get a grip on yourself girl....remember God's got you and Adam, only believe! And I said what I was thinking out loud, but if only to reassure myself...."I believe, I do God!"

When I walked into Adam's room, I was surprised... what in the world!? Adam's color was off, his normally tan and dark skin now had an ashen color and he had a machine, that looked as if it were breathing for him. Adam did not look well at all! It was then that I heard a knock at the door..."Mrs. Anna, it's Jacqueline." "Jacqueline, I was only gone for a short while...why does Adam's color look so off? Why does he look so ashen?" "Mrs. Anna, Adam's oxygen saturation dropped, he's now on a Bipap machine, which will help with his oxygen saturation. We don't know why his O2 saturation dropped but the Bipap machine will help with that and the doctor ordered a test; an ABG blood test and a lactic acid that will tell us if Adam's condition is worsening. Dr. Bliven ordered something to help keep him sedated and calm. I tried to call you at home, but I couldn't get an answer and I didn't want to call you on your cell phone, in case you were en route to the hospital, you know?" "I appreciate that Jacqueline! I feel comfortable that he is getting the best care and that Dr. Bliven's finger is on the pulse of everything that is going on with Adam. I really appreciate all of you!" I couldn't help myself; maybe because I was so emotional anyway or maybe I just needed a hug, but I grabbed Jacqueline and hugged her tight. I heard a tremor in her voice as she grabbed my hand and looked me in the eyes...."Mrs. Anna, never, ever forget that God is right here, in the midst. He is the Great Comforter, the Great Healer, and the Great Consoler!" I grasped her hand tightly and couldn't finish my words but nodded in agreement, with tears running down the side of both cheeks. "Call me if you need anything and I'll be right in, okay?" "I promise!" I sat down in the chair, and watched Adam intently, hand over my mouth, while I cried softly, praying and hoping that my hand would smother, condense the sound of my crying.....

Adam

"Adam, wake up!" My head felt so foggy....and as I opened my eyes....it took a full few minutes to focus on the Person in front of me. "Adam, it is I and I am here for you!" "Who are you? Do I know you?" "Adam, you know Me....It is I, the One that loves you. I am here for you because I love you and because of a special request by a special, wonderful young man." "What? What is going on....why does my head hurt so badly...ugh it feels like a migraine!" And with that I felt the warmth of a touch to my forehead...."Is that better?" My eyes were focused and surprisingly my headache was gone! Standing by my bed was a Man...but He was different. He glowed outward from every cell of His body....He glowed as bright as the Sun! He had a short but full beard, dark skin and was wearing what I can only describe as a robe with a golden sash at the waist....but His eyes were what stood out. They were so warm, so inviting, understanding, and they reflected so much love, so much tenderness. "I'm sorry, but who are You?" "Adam, I am He and your Abel, whom I love, is with Me now. I am here because of My love for you, because I care and because you need to know many truths." I couldn't quite grasp his response and blurted out instantaneously...."Have I died? Are you Jesus? What is going on here?" "He smiled and laughed softly. "No, Adam you have not died and yes I am He. I want to take you on a journey but first you must trust and believe Me.""Where are we going? I don't understand this at all. It's been so long since I've thought of You, prayed to You...." "I know this, but that doesn't mean that My love for you has lessened any....I have loved you even before We made all of this, even before time began. If you will trust and believe and take My hand, I will take you on a journey to where your Abel is; can you do this?" Still unsure, and with the thought of Abel, my boy, on my mind, I grabbed His hand tightly and shook my head with a nod, "Yes, I trust and believe You!" And the moment I grabbed His hand, I felt myself leave my body and travelling upward.....I looked back in disbelief as I saw myself still in bed, with my eyes closed hooked up to machines and tubes. As we travelled upward, I looked around and saw that we were in a tunnel. It felt like I was in the center (eye) of a tornado, being pulled upward through the windy tunnel but as we travelled upward, scenes from my life were presented as though on IMAX. I saw myself at 5 years old, crying because my mother scolded me for stealing a candy bar at the local drugstore and I felt, actually felt my feelings at that time and my mother's feelings of disappointment, and hurt. I then saw another scene in which I had helped one of our neighbors, who had gotten sick and couldn't work while on his treatments, mow his grass and clean up his yard and I felt such gratitude from this neighbor, such love for my actions. I could actually feel what my neighbor felt for me....it was amazing! I continued to watch different scenes from my life; my graduation from high school, my wedding day, the birth of Abel....amazing that I could feel what the other's were feeling in those different scenes of my life. I could feel the immense joy, the complete love of my mom, my dad and Anna at the birth of Abel. It was at this point that we stopped in the tunnel and He spoke to me..."Adam, all of these scenes are from your life. This is your life in review, up until this point in your life." We then turned and watch (as in a full, gigantic movie screen) several other moments in my life....when

I stood up for another kid in grammar school that was being bullied and the immense gratitude that he felt towards me because of this act, the moment that I found out Abel had died and the feelings associated with that including Anna's feelings of betrayal, hurt and disappointment when I wouldn't open up to her and acknowledge those immense feelings of grief, of loss. There were several scenes of me inebriated at my house, crying in silence, being hurtful and angry with any and everyone....and I felt such an overwhelming sense of shame; almost unbearable! "I am so ashamed! What a mess I've made of my life since I've lost Abel; we've lost Abel." And He turned to face me and softly grabbed both of my arms and said "Adam, your loss was great, but you have to know that your Abel is with Me. He is safe, he is in a wonderful place.....His true home; a place that I've prepared for all that seek Me with fellowship, with true love in their hearts. But I've come to you because of a special request; a request from Abel himself. He truly wants you to heal; from the hurt, the open wounds that you carry daily. He wants peace for you in your life, but especially in your heart!" It was then that we were standing by a crystal blue stream, whose surface, softly glowed as if diamonds were scattered up its surface, and the bankhead was covered with the most beautiful flowers I have ever seen! Wonderful maroon, periwinkle, golden yellow, bright red, deep rich purple flowers that clustered to-gether; readymade for a bouquet. I could hear the most beautiful music, soft and subtle, and even the flowers and the tall dark green grass seemed to sway as if in a dance with the music. Everything seemed alive; even the trees seemed to lean toward Him as He walked past them; as if bowing in respect and reverence. "I have someone that wants to see you and he is so excited! Enjoy this Gift for it comes from a place of Absolute Love. Love from Me and love from your Abel!" I then turned away from Him and standing in front of me was my boy....my sweet wonderful boy, exactly as he always was, but something was different? My knees were as weak as water and I fell down on them and held out my arms and Abel ran to me and embraced me. "Oh daddy, I'm so glad you are here. Jesus gave both of us this special Gift! I have missed you!" I couldn't get my words out....all I could do was nod my head in agreement; acknowledging this great gift and acknowledging how much I missed my boy! Abel and I stood up...."Daddy, let's go for a walk. Jesus is that okay?" "Of course it is, my boy, I'll meet you in a little while" and with that He walked away. "Abel, I've missed you so much! I didn't handle it very well....I've messed up so bad!" "Daddy, there is nothing that you have done or could do that would ever make me love you any less! But daddy, I wanted you to see that I am safe, and although I miss you, mom, grammie, and all of my friends....I am happy. I know that one day we will all be together again." "But how do I go on living without you? How do I get through each day? How do I brea...I couldn't even get out my question without a long pause...How do I breathe each day?" "Oh daddy, I sure do love you so much! You are the best daddy ever!" Abel grabbed my hand and we continued to walk by the stream, he quietly with me, with me watching my boy....memorizing everything about him. I heard a bark and saw a dog beating a path down through the grass and looked at Abel...."Is that...? No, it can't be, not after all of this time? Is that my old dog, Beau?" I had owned a dog, when I was a little boy named Beau; a Springer Spaniel. He slept with me, played with me, did everything with me, but he had gotten out of our front door and before I could catch him, ran in front of a car and was hit. We then took him to the vet, and because of his injuries, the vet advised that the most humane thing to do would be to put him down. I can remember the pain, the crying, the anguish over losing my best friend; Beau, yet even today, still so fresh. "Daddy, it is! When I first got here, Beau was one of the first to greet me. He's such a good boy!" "How can that be? I didn't think that animals had souls, that animals made it to Heaven." "Oh yes, daddy, Jesus told me that nothing is ever lost." Beau ran up to me and as I bent down to pet him, jumping up in my arms, licking my face all over. Beau did his little happy dance (that's what we all called it) jumping around in circles in front of me. "Daddy, he stays with me all the time. I take good care of him!" I soaked up all of this wonderful.....all of this Gift, yes, every little moment of it!

As we were playing with Beau, I felt a Presence behind me and turned around to see Him; Jesus, coming down the path to join us. "I see that you and Beau have gotten re-acquainted as well." As He walked up to us and bent down to pet Beau....I studied Him. I had been so wrapped up in my own grief that I had lost the ability to actually look around me, look and study the important things, the important ones in my life. His very Being exuded love, compassion and a serene peace....I could feel His love for me, it felt so wonderful....it filled me to the brim with joy and contentment. He exuded a glow, a glow that seemed to come from His innermost

Being down to His fingertips and His eyes.....they were a mixture of blue and green and reflected a most compassionate, most loving, and forgiving Father.....yes, I remembered Him. I searched for Him when I was younger, I wanted what He was offering....and I stood there studying Him, grateful that He did not give up on me, never stopped loving me.....always in the background ready for me to come back Home. He was my Home....

"Abel, would it be alright if I spoke to your daddy just for a moment? I promise, it will only be a short while. Why don't you take Beau into the park and play with him and we'll meet you there?" "Okay, come on Beau...come on boy! Love you daddy." As we watched him and Beau walk away, I could not stop the tears.... the tears that I tried to numb with alcohol, the tears that I pressed down, the tears that I traded for a bag full of bitterness, and hurt! The tears that flowed now were not from grief, but from a knowing that my boy,,that all things are kept....nothing is ever lost and non-existent after their use....the Lord, with His mercy and compassion has showed me that ALL things matter to Him. Why was I worried about Abel? Maybe I wasn't even worried but was just so consumed with the actual thought that while I was on this earth, I would never see him in his physical form again. I know that grief is so different for everybody....each person's response to grief is so different. How do I reconcile this idea of never seeing my son again, while I am living? How do I go on day in and day out without him? How do I remember to breathe without him? As if queued by my questions, Jesus turned around to me and spoke to me...."Adam, do you know that you are loved? Do you know what this Place is?"

"I do! This is Heaven. But I've made so many mist,"....
and I couldn't finish my sentence....I felt so ashamed!
"Adam, is there anything, anything in the world that
Abel could have done that would make you love him
any less? Would you or could you ever give up on him or
stop loving him?" "Well no, never. He is my child, he's
my everything." "That is how We feel about you. There
is absolutely nothing that you could do that would or
could ever make Us stop loving you, nothing! Do you
remember the scenes of your life while we were on our
way here to Heaven? What was the constant theme
throughout these images....what was the most important understanding that you received from all of these
images?" "Well, for every instance that I did something
I wasn't supposed to or that was wrong, I felt the actual
hurt, the pain and the disappointment felt by others
that I interacted with at those times in my life." "You
are right, but more importantly, remember the times,
when you helped others.....when you did an act of goodness or sacrificed for love for others.....remember how
good that you felt? Those times in your life...in everyone's life are THE MOST IMPORTANT.....those times
are when you show a piece of the Divine, a piece of Us,
within you! Your grief, as all grief is, is an intimate feeling, an acknowledgement of the love you felt, the loss
that you are experiencing,.....it is a testament to the
love that you have for Abel. It is a process and it must
be considered and given its rightful moment....it must
be dealt with, it cannot be assuaged or pressed down....
it doesn't work that way. Grief knows no bounds and
your grief for Abel must be acknowledged and claimed
for you to move forward. Do you understand this? My
Father grieved....for Me on My journey to the Cross. A

tremendous grief, an all consuming grief! He knew that I would be with Him in Heaven and yet He grieved. He understood the sacrifice that I gave willingly and yet He still grieved. I promise you, your grief is felt by Us. We understand!" And with that comment, He grabbed me softly and held me close, so tight that I had to catch my breath, so tight that I felt maybe the pieces that were scattered within me, could be put back together again. And I cried, I cried hard...and let out a wounded howl, which surprised me but not Him. He understood! After I had spent my entire self crying, I drew back and He looked me in the eye....."Adam you are so loved and you will get through this. Nothing ever, ever happens that We are not aware of, We are with you on this journey of grief." "But why did Abel have to go? Why did you take him?" "Adam, every person on earth has a determined number of days...every single one, even you. We knew that Abel's time on earth would not be long, but you and all others that believe in Us, spend time in prayer to Us, love Us, let Us lead, direct your life, give Us your very all.....will never have to bear the pain of separation, the sting of death...for in Me you will find everlasting life. I have here a place prepared for all that are in My family, every single one." As I set down in the grass, Jesus sat down with me. I understood and while it would still be difficult, probably for the rest of my days on earth, I understood.

I understood the complete and absolute sacrifice given for all of us! While I had lost my only child and son, I could and couldn't completely fathom the supreme sacrifice given freely by Jesus on the road to the Cross and I couldn't fathom how much God and the Holy Spirit must have grieved on that Day of Absolution, the

Day of Abundance given so freely to every one of us! I felt at that moment such a serene all encompassing peace, a knowing that everything would be alright, that me and Anna could make it through this. As I looked over at Jesus, I caught Him staring at me...."My child, please know that your Abel is deeply loved and taken care of by us, I promise you with My Absolute Word of Truth. From the moment he entered Heaven, he has known nothing but peace, love, fulfillment, and contentment. Remember the words of Exodus 33 verse 14...."*My Presence will go with you, and I will give you rest.*" "Peace, true peace, the kind that stills the restless, wandering soul can only come through Us. This peace will warm and protect your heart, specifically on those nights, when all is quiet and you are left to your own dangerous and self-destructive thoughts of what could have been, what should have been, and what should be....this is the absolute truth!"

"I know that you have struggled, you've lost your way....but today is a new day! A new day to start fresh, a new day to begin over again!" As I was looking at Jesus, I caught movement out of the corner of my eye and saw Abel walking down the path, with a child on either side of him. I looked at Jesus and I think I saw Him wink at me and smile! "Daddy, I have two special people that I'd love for you to meet!" Abel was holding hands with a little girl and a little boy...."Daddy, this is Noah." And with that introduction, Noah ran up to me and hugged my neck. "And Daddy, this is Kathleen Ella." As I looked over at Noah, it was almost as if I were looking at a younger picture of myself,... curly thick, black hair, chocolate brown eyes, and those deep, pitted dimples in each of his little cheeks. And as

I looked over at Kathleen Ella, with her sky blue eyes, blonde hair and her sporadic tiny freckles that dotted her cheeks....I could see Anna. Kathleen Ella came up to me slowly, but studying my face, she reached down and hugged my neck and gave me a kiss on my cheek. "Abel, are these your new friends here?" Abel then exchanged a knowing look with Jesus and Jesus intercepted for him...."Adam, these are Abel's brother and sister!" "Wait, what, how can that be?""These are your children....Kathleen Ella will come first, and then two years later, Noah will come along" and Jesus softly touched my shoulder and squeezed it and with a sparkle of a tear in his eye, he said...."We love you and Anna and only wish wonderful, happy lives for you! Life will and can be hard at times and trials will come; some to stay for awhile, but take heart Adam, persevere for I am here at all times and only a prayer away. Perseverance, faith, trust and love are needed in this world today. The world today is not the world that Adam and Eve were made for; it runs rampant with sin, ego, self-destruction, self-promotion, hostility, and hate but there is also an abundance (as I've seen it and felt it) of love, self-sacrifice, true humility, compassion and tolerance. Hold onto these attributes for they truly will change you; they will break you, mold you, change you and enlighten your very essence; your soul." "I will truly try, Jesus but what if I fall, what if I fold when these trials come; I don't want to lose my chance to come back here, to be with Abel?" "My son, you can never earn your way into Heaven! The Gift of Heaven is freely given to all but if you only ask Us to come into your life; give the most valuable part of yourself to Us; your heart. For you see it is the heart that we look at of the man or woman; it is a most precious part of the human anatomy. The heart determines actions, reactions, words spoken, love manifested, sacrifice, and compassion but without any of these, the heart is but a stone. A useless piece of stone! What good does a heart when it is but only stone; absolutely nothing! Do not ever let circumstances, losses, situations determine the condition of your heart; give all of those to Me, for I can bear those burdens, they are as light as air." As I sat there talking with Him, I felt such a release; a calm, a stillness that permeated into my very being! "Look at all three of your Gifts standing here before you! What a blessed man that you are!""I know, I'm so happy"....I couldn't get the words out...and I had to pause, to gain my composure and start my sentence again...."I know, I'm so happy and I'm so very blessed!" And with that Jesus stood up and grabbed my hand to help me up to my feet. "Adam, it is almost time for you to go and I know that you will want to speak with Abel. I will take Noah and Kathleen Ella with me. "How about going for a walk with me? Kathleen does that sound good to you? Noah how about you?" Jesus picked up both of them and turning they waved..."Bye bye daddy! Love you! Love you!" and with a smile as big as Heaven, Jesus turned and started down the path, speaking to both of them as I could see His head turn from right to left. It was then that I heard a huge bellow of a laugh come from Jesus and then saw Noah and Kathleen giggle, with Kathleen covering her mouth and Noah pressing his cheek to Jesus face...

"Daddy, I love you so much!" And with that Abel grabbed my hand and we held hands as he walked me back towards the bottom of the valley. The walk was quiet, reflective, and healing for me! As we came to the edge of the forest in the valley, Abel turned to face me and spoke..."Daddy, I am happy here and I'm taken care of but even though this Place is a place of joy, of love, of family....I see you Daddy, and I feel the hurt and anger in your heart. Promise me that you will let all of that go...you will enjoy your life? And I will always be waiting right here when it is your time to leave....or mom's turn, or grammie's turn...I will be here waiting." As I cupped the side of his face...I could only say out loud exactly what I was thinking...."When in the world did you grow up? Who is this young man? When did you become wiser than your old man?" Abel looked up at me with a small smile but I could see the tears glistening in his eyes and as I dropped my hand from his face, he wiped his eyes with his forearm and cleared his throat...."Daddy, Jesus is the reason. I have spent so much time with Him and He explains things...all things so easily even a kid like me can understand them. He's wonderful daddy....just like you!" I could see his bottom lip start to quiver and I softly pulled him to me and hugged him for what seemed an eternity, but not long enough for either of us...

"Daddy, you do know that Jesus was (is) a carpenter?" "Yes, I do remember this." "Well, I have a surprise for you! Me and Jesus have been working on something for a little while and it's finally finished and I wanted you to have it. I mean, I did a lot of the work, but He guided me, helped me with it." "Abel, that is wonderful! Come and show me where you have it!" Abel grabbed my hand and as we walked around the edge of the woods, I saw a small shop. It was completely made of cedar, with an opening or walkway in the front and a huge window on both sides. I could smell the cedar! "Daddy, this is my shop! Jesus made it for me and it's where I come sometimes and work on my projects. "Abel this is great....do you work by yourself?" "No, hardly ever. I have a best friend, Frankie, who always comes and helps me. Come on in and let me show you what we've been working on!" As I walked into the shed, I could smell the sweet smell of Cedar wood and I saw birdhouses....so many, too many to count. Each made with all different kinds of woods; cedar, pine, olive, spruce or poplar and they were all of various shapes and sizes. Each different, so specific; detailed and crafted with love. "Daddy, blue birds are my favorite bird and their birdhouses have to be specific; the right diameter in the opening, the exact and right location of the opening; they are quite particular with their houses. Daddy, I guess the birds do like my houses; I have them scattered all over Heaven. And sometimes I just sit and watch them! Okay now daddy, I need you to close your eyes and hold out your hand, it's a surprise!" And I squinted my eyes tightly close and held out my hand and felt Abel place a small box into my hand. "Okay, open your eyes now daddy!!" I opened my eyes and looked down at my hand and there in my hand was the most exquisite, detailed, smoothed, polished wood box. This box was made of olive wood, the wood was knotted on all four corners of the box, with a gold clasp in the center of the box. It was amazing to see, but more specifically what was amazing, was the amount of detailed handiwork obviously put into the craftsmanship of the box. On all four sides were intricate carvings of Abel and me together; but these were actual color printed carvings that seem to be imbedded within the wood work! "Daddy, open it up!" And Abel pointed at the clasp in the center of the box. And as I opened it up, I saw a small, perfectly carved wooden heart with Abel's name carved on it. "Oh Abel, this is the absolute best gift, but I mean, how did you do this? The pictures on the side, they look like actual photos, how in the world did you imbed these within the wood?" "Daddy, Jesus helped me with those! At first I thought it wouldn't be possible, but Jesus told me that all things are possible! He asked me to give it to Him and He would work on that portion of the box for me, so He took the box for a short time and when I got it back, the pictures were on all four sides!" I reached in and pulled out the heart with Abel's name engraved and kissed it. "Daddy, I put the heart in the box; to remind you that I'm always with you, that I'm taken care of, but most importantly, for you to remember to guard your heart daddy. Keep it safe, keep it protected, keep it guarded. Jesus explained to me just as He did you, how important the heart is and Jesus always watches the heart of everyone. It's so important daddy....Please daddy, whenever you feel sad or you feel alone.....give your heart and your troubles to Jesus!" Abel grabbed me by my waist and hugged me tightly, tightly enough that I felt all the broken pieces fall away. All the hardness, all the self-destruction, all the worries, even the all-consuming rage, hurt and bitterness. It all fell away; each, hard, destructive and negative feeling fell away and it felt good! It was such a release and I felt so light, a moment of nothing short of sheer joy! "Abel, I promise you, I will take this and keep it close to me,,,always, son! Always!"

I slowly opened my eyes, my arms extended, still

hugging Abel, when I heard Anna's voice. "Adam, honey are you okay? You're crying and your, your...left arm....you've lifted it up without any help! Adam, are you okay?" "Abel, oh Abel!" "What did you say? Did you say..."Abel?" I nodded my head in agreement and Anna covered her mouth with her hand....great, large tears dropping down on the front of my gown. I was changed, different and this wasn't a change of mood or a change of feelings....this change I felt from the heart. This change felt good, it felt right. "Adam what is this?"....as she slowly opened up my hand and found the box. Anna gave me that knowing look....that look that didn't need any words, no explanation....only a wonderful acknowledgement of each for our wonderful Gifts.....our "Visit" and our keepsakes given to us by our Loving, Compassionate God and our boy, with a heart as big as the universe! "Oh Adam, let me go get the nurse! I'll be right back, okay?" I nodded my head; tears still streaming down my face and I said a quiet prayer of thanks to Him! It was all that mattered at that moment...a prayer of gratitude, a prayer of purpose, a prayer of love!

From that day on, everything changed. No longer did I feel the effects of the stroke as I was freely able to move my left arm and leg and gone was the lopsided smile. I stayed for another 3 days, gradually stepping down from the unit to a floor bed and then I was discharged home. And the perpetual need for alcohol, it was gone, absolutely and completely gone! I never thirsted for alcohol again and if the truth be absolutely known, I never tasted alcohol again, ever. While it may be okay for some, I knew that alcohol was my Achilles heel, my weakness and I never even indulged the possibility of opening up that old wound ever again. Oh on special occasions, or dinners with friends, Anna would have the occasionally glass of wine,... it never bothered me or tempted me. Amazing isn't it, that when a hurt is healed how absolutely every other thing within one's life begins to heal? This marvelous, wonderful, amazing life is like that! But I know the real reason for the healing that began in my very soul.....it was the Son of God and my little boy. The Gift given to me by Jesus, much as the Gift of the Cross, could never be repaid. Did I deserve such a gift? Absolutely not, I was in the absolute worst position a person could be in.... hopeless, bitter, angry, hurt, and self-destructive...but that's when Grace stepped in and Grace had a name and its name was Jesus! What could I possibly do to ever repay for this gift.....I've thought on this at great length and came to the conclusion that I could take the Master at His word; live my life in a way that honors Him, ask daily for forgiveness for known and unknown sins, but most importantly let Him be Lord of my life in all things.

Oh and I kept that box close....that wonderful box! That box that exemplified, personified the love between me and my son. The box made from Love and given in Love by my sweet boy and Jesus! Jesus didn't have to, but He understood, He understands the human condition, the heart breaks, the losses, the helplessness....and I will be forever grateful to Him! That box for me was Hope.....Hope so desperately needed and freely given....

Anna

When I found Adam reaching; reaching up with his arms into the air....I was concerned, I was struck cold with an all consuming fear, the fear that freezes your blood. Yeah that kind of fear! But when I leaned down and heard him say "Abel", I knew that something was different. And when I saw the cascade of tears falling down like a waterfall, into the creases of his cheeks,....I knew something profound had happened, some extraordinary! Dr. Bliven was amazed with just how quick Adam's recovery took place. We were able to take him off of the oxygen mask, only to see his oxygen saturation remain stable at 98-99% and his blood pressure, well his blood pressure was as good as mine was and remained stable with no spikes, no elevations in blood pressure. But let's talk about his left arm, his left leg and the left side of his face; amazingly there were no residual effects from his stroke. Now anyone can chalk this up to the medication that he received within the first three critical hours of his stroke but I believe differently. And I can say this without hesitancy, because from that day forward, Adam never, ever touched another drop of alcohol nor did he want to; he never had the desire for it again. It took him a few days before he could finish the story of Abel to me; but he told me the story of Abel, Noah, Kathleen Ella and Jesus. He told me everything and I believe him. I always will because I know that on a lonely, lost night not too long ago; I had a story, a magnificent story filled to the brim with the Gift of Grace. Even as we compared our stories, the common theme and message given; we both are still in a state of complete awe, at the magnitude of His message and His amazing love for me and Adam; but really quite truthfully; His absolute and true love for all of us...each and every one of us! A story that I will hold close to my heart until I see Jesus and Abel again; a story that gives me peace, serene calmness, absolute joy and a fervor that cannot be quelled for our Lord Jesus Christ! Did me or Adam deserve this gift, not at all, even on our very best days, but that's when Jesus stepped in with His magnificent Grace and changed our hearts forever.

Our life continued on, much happier and blessed than we could ever imagine and just as Jesus told us; Kathleen Ella came first with Noah coming two years later. Kathleen Ella nor Noah remember Heaven at all; they never speak of it. Oh they both go to church, they know about Jesus; they say their prayers and they believe, but they don't remember, but how funny that sometimes things are said or happen that will stop a person right in their tracks. As I'm cutting the corners off of their peanut butter and jelly sandwiches, I hear Kathleen call me in the other room, with Noah chiming in also. "Mommy, come here we need to tell you something." "I'm coming!" As I walk into the dining room, Noah is trying his best to write his name as Kathleen is coloring in her favorite unicorn coloring book. "Mommy, I think that we need to tell you something, something important." With Noah adding...."Yeah, it's important, it really is!" "Okay, I'm all ears" I say as I grab both of my ears and pull on them and they both look seriously at each other and break out in a laugh. Kathleen starts...."Mommy, I think that me and Noah picked you and daddy to be our mommy and daddy." "Why do you say that baby?" "I just feel like we did!" Looking at both of them, Kathleen with her soft crystal blue eyes and Noah with his deep rich chocolate brown eyes, I know that this right here is a God Thing. You know those moments when in the midst of the chaos that is life, you are given a Gift; a moment of wonder and awe, and you think to yourself in that quiet moment.....WOW, this word, this act, this feeling came from another place! That was this moment...and I knew it as I rubbed first Kathleen's cheek and then Noah's cheek. "I think you did too and I'm so happy that you chose us to be your mommy and daddy!"

As the years went by, and Kathleen and Noah grew into adulthood, our family unit enlarged to include our cherished in-laws, aunts, cousins, uncles, grandmothers, grandfathers, and friends that became family to us. Noah married a wonderful girl, Mary Grace and gave us 3 cherished jewels that we call our grandchildren. Kathleen Ella married a wonderful guy, Samuel and gave us 4 cherished jewels that we call our grandchildren. Kathleen grew up to become a teacher; she works with those extra special children that God graces all of us with; those on the autism spectrum. Noah became a Pastor, and works in his spare time with kids that are less fortunate than others, providing them with a sense of purpose, a sense of belonging. Both of them have good lives; both of them are happy with their life choices.

Christmas time is magical and this year, I wanted everything to be perfect. Our large den had the real tree, that Adam and Noah had purchased from a friend, and it was decorated in reds and golds with red and gold streamers bursting out at the top of the tree and large pieces of glittery gold ribbon woven around the base of the tree. This was our special tree. Every ornament that hung on its limbs were handmade by loved ones; my mom, Noah, Kathleen Ella. Huge ornaments made with hand painted scenes (courtesy of Noah) on whirled glass, a huge array of crocheted ornaments (bells, crosses, and elves) (courtesy of my mom) and huge wooden ornaments with scenes engraved of the Baby Jesus, Mother Mary and Joseph, and family pictures of long ago; including a picture of Abel on Christmas Day when he was about 3 years old. Poinsettias lined our front vestibule in light greens and magnificent reds. Within one of the wider halls that lead to the bedrooms (on the bottom floor), was the manger scene complete with a life sized Mary, Joseph and Baby Jesus. Adam made the wooden bed for Baby Jesus, complete with straw. In the sun room, we placed our white tree, clothed in all blue and wrapped with silver ribbons from the head to the foot of the tree. This tree was decorated by our grandchildren every year; it has become quite the event! I ordered little doll sized elves that I decorated each of the bottom of the trees with and as I tried not to laugh; I explained to our grandchildren....."You have to watch these little elves...they are mischievous! ...You never know what they are up to!" Noah's little boy Robert David looked up at me, with a face full of concern; "Nana, do you think that they are watching us, even when we be bad? I tried to hide my smile as I told him...."I don't know? Maybe, that's why you have to be on your best behavior or they spill the beans to Santa!" Robert David looked at me with a half-smile and said...."I'll be a good boy, Nana!" As Christmas Eve continued and it became later; Adam said for all to hear; "Well, I'm thinking that it's about time for the telling of the Christmas Story. Is everyone ready? Do you have your hot chocolate and your cookies ready?" All of the little ones squealed with delight....with each talking over the over one; Nicole shouted out...."I'm ready", while Joseph grabbing his hot chocolate says...."Hold on, I'm almost ready!" We had begun the tradition of the Christmas Story a year or two before and the little ones loved it! We were always bombarded with several questions....."Why didn't they have a room at the Inn? Didn't they know that the baby was Jesus? Why didn't they go to a hospital, Nana?" And as always on cue, the older grandchildren would respond to the questions,,,"There wasn't a hospital back then" or They didn't know who baby Jesus was at that time".....with an exaggerated, knowing eye roll and a look at me and papa to confirm that they were indeed right in their summation......

As the kids were starting to get tired, worn down and rubbing their little eyes; Noah and Mary Grace along with Kathleen Ella and Samuel started packing up the children's gifts and goodies and we started with the goodbyes. As I look over at my children and all of my grandchildren; my heart skips a beat....my heart is so full! As Adam and I help them with all of their stuff to the car and everyone spreads the love; with tight hugs and a kiss, I realized just how blessed we are! I look over at Adam and we both smile; a smile full of contentment, peace, and absolute love! We are so blessed.....

After I had finished cleaning up the living room, the den and the kitchen....I sit down on the love seat in the den and Adam calls to me from the living room....."Yes honey, what's up?..."Hey babe, what do you want to watch on TV tonight?"....Adam asks as he grabs the remote control. "I'm not really feeling it tonight. I think

I'm going to lie down for awhile. I have the start of a bad headache....feels like I'm trying to get a tooth-ache....my jaw sure feels sore!" "Okay, call me if you need me; I think I'm going to try and watch that movie I've been wanting to watch." As I put on my nightgown, and crawled under the bed covers, Adam came into our bedroom, and gave me a soft, sweet kiss, pulling my covers up and settling me into bed before turning off the bedside lamp and walking out, closing the door behind him. But then I hear him pause and turn around and poke his head into the door and whisper......"Happy 65th Birthday, beautiful! I love you very much!" "I love you too honey, thank you!" and I blow him a kiss in the air.

I am officially 65 years young....wow, I can hardly believe it! Wasn't I just 32 yesterday with two small little ones at my side? It seemed to take forever to turn 21 but then and since then, the years have flown by! Time stands still for no one, you can be sure! Oh I sure hope that headache medicine kicks in soon! My best friend, Rhonda had made me a cake for my birthday.... my most favorite; German Chocolate! I didn't want a lot of fuss about my birthday and wanted to focus on the little ones for their Christmas and we had decided as a family to celebrate my birthday on the next week-end. But Rhonda, as always, showed up at my front door with her German Chocolate birthday cake and it was so wonderful...spending time with her and trying to get her recipe but ultimately forgetting to ask before she left our house. I need to remember to get her reci-pe tomorrow when we meet for lunch. She's been one of my best friends since the eighth grade; wow, eighth grade.....!! I love her so much! Such a wonderful woman of God! I am so blessed that she is in my life! Oh I can't hardly keep my eyes open......they feel so heavy! I can hear the television down the hall and Adam laughing every so often...I might have to sit down and try to watch that movie tomorrow! We have been wanting to watch it together for about a week....since it came out, but something always comes up, especially here around the holidays. As I roll over in the bed and pull the covers up over my shoulders, I say a prayer of thanks, of gratitude to the Lord and a prayer for forgiveness! I whisper in the darkness to the Lord, knowing that He is right here listening to me...."Please send my Abel a kiss for me and let him know he is missed so much".....and I feel a warm tear sliding down the side of my left cheek...rolling into my ear. As I go over in my mind all of the activities of the day, the fun, the laughter and the love....I feel warmth, I feel a perpetual smile...a wonderment at this marvelous life. So wonderful the life that me and Adam have made together....we are so fortunate...we are so blessed. Uh, this headache seems to be easing off....thank goodness and my eyes are so heavy....Wait what is that bright light? "Whose there? Who is that?" I heard a vaguely familiar voice answer in the darkness...."Mommy, it's me,,,it's your Abel and I've come to take you home. Please mommy, take my hand........

PREFACE

There are so many reasons why I wrote this book. This book came to me with an idea based on Grace, Hope and Faith. **Grace**, defined by me, *is God's ability to love all of us through our pain, through our circumstances, our situations, our defeats, our shortcomings.....through all situations that inevitably will rise up during our lifetime.* Grace is the Gift of Absolute Love given by our Father in Heaven!

Hope, defined by me, *is God's ability to reassure us that He is the same today, tomorrow and every single day of our lives.* This reassurance can manifest in the most unusual ways; a visit from a friend, a phone call from a loved one, just an I Love You from a special someone, all needed and provided at just the right precise times in our lives. Every single person living needs this reassurance; this hope!

Faith, defined by me, *is our ability, in even the most trying times of our lives, to walk on the water with Christ. To defy the odds, to believe in Him sometimes when we can't feel Him, or see Him working* *within our lives.* Faith is holding onto that Mustard seed; holding it so tight within the palm of your hand, knowing that this Faith will have long term, far reaching effects in our daily walk with our Lord!

ACKNOWLEDGEMENTS

First and foremost, I have to give all of the credit to our Lord, Jesus Christ, for without Him, I am nothing. I fall short every single day in my walk with Him, but His Grace and Goodness are more than sufficient. I first came into an awareness of Jesus, when I was but 12 years, but as I grew older; my attentions, my goals, my life took a turn and I was headed straight down "that long wide road of destruction" that so many travel in their lives. As I've gotten older, and I've looked back....there are so many times that I can see NOW where Christ was working within my life. As a victim of a motor vehicle accident (February 3, 1995), with significant injuries including but not limited to; cardiac contusions, bad concussion, a lacerated spleen, and a damaged diaphragm, I found myself awakened while trapped in the vehicle by two Good Samaritan gentlemen, and sub sequentially cut out by the jaws of life. Fortunately my daughter, did not suffer any physical effects other than a scratch on her ear and her ankle! But it was the story that this little girl (my little girl of

4 years old) told me that made me catch my breath! For you see, while I was unconscious, Candice, who was awake, saw (in her words, not mine) a "glittery lady holding your head, mama!" Wow, my first words were...."Candice, did she have wings?"....followed by "No, mama, but she was beautiful and as she was holding your head, pointed for me to go out the back of the vehicle!" Now obviously she spoke and told me this as a four year old would tell a story and I am putting grown up words in its stead, but the meaning and the Grace behind this incredible Visit does not lose its significance, by no means! For you see at this point in my life, if I had not survived this crash....am I sure that I would have gone to Heaven to be with Jesus? The answer would be a resounding NO! This is Grace....Grace given when it is the least deserved and I am so grateful for His Grace!

Or we can talk about the single Mom, who worked two jobs, to make ends meet but even this did not suffice! There are so many single Moms out there and I have the upmost respect for every single one of them.... those that fight the fight alone, those that wear threadbare clothes so their children can get their necessities, those that go to bed hungry just so their child(ren) have enough to eat, those that worry constantly because $5 or even $1 can overdraw their bank account,,,,...Yes, I have lived all of these scenarios...every single one! But let's talk about Grace and Hope again....This single Mom (me) pulls into a grocery store parking lot to pick up some crackers (snacks), and a 2 liter drink, feeling desperate and so discouraged and she (I) offered up a desperate prayer like this....."God, please, please if you hear any of my prayers or if my prayers are going past my ceiling....please give me a sign! Let me know that You're still there!" And this single Mom (again, this is Me) walks into the grocery story....no one really in the parking lot except a young guy standing at the doors, I get my box of crackers and my 2 liter drink, and as I'm walking out to my car, I'm approached from behind and tapped on my right shoulder...which startled me..."Hey there! Let me ask you a question, ma'am, do you love the Lord God with all of your heart....with all that you are?" I answer with a "Yes!" Then this gentleman responds with "Then say His Name!!" Now this gentleman had no brochures, no invitation to any of our local churches, absolutely nothing in his hands....but he had a message to me from Him, the most Precious One, the Reason for all of us...Yes, I would say that was definitely a sign...a neon sign sent from above, a sign that was SO NEEDED and was the reassurance that stayed my restless, discouraged heart! Thank You Jesus!

***This book is dedicated to ALL Mothers and Fathers that have lost a child. My hope is that in reading this book, these Mothers and Fathers find a measure of peace, a measure of love, a measure of hope.

**Thank you to my wonderful husband; Cameron Floyd. This book is dedicated to him! He continues in his walk with the Lord daily and he is such an inspiration to me; always! He is and will always be my absolute best friend! We have a good life and I cherish, adore and love him more than I could ever put into words..... There aren't enough words to express my respect or my love for him.

I would also like to thank my Sister-In-Love; Audrey Streit, for without her encouragement, her love, I would never have attempted this book! She is a wonderful, loving, servant of God! My love for her knows no bounds....

My Children....what can I say about them....they are everything to me. My days are so much sweeter whenever I talk with them, find out what's going within their lives, laugh with them, and let them know that they are loved, so very much! Justin, Ludie and Candice, you are the sun, moon and stars! All of you are such wonderful human beings, and I am so grateful that you are mine. There is not a mother, that has ever lived or that ever will live, that could not be prouder of each of you. Each of you are compassionate, loving, caring, giving, so funny, fiercely protective of each other and family, and loyal to each other and family.....The world is blessed because you live in it!!! I love you all!

My Grandchildren...You are the Universe to me! The love that I have for Kathleen Ella and Noah could never be measured or understood. They are perfect, they are loved, they are cherished....each and every moment spent with them is like Heaven here on Earth! There are not enough words in the English language, that could ever help me describe just exactly what they mean to me....none. This is the absolute truth! I love you both so much!

And I would like to thank my own brothers and sisters. I have 3 brothers (Bryan, Jason and Joseph), and 2 sisters (Teresa and Dawn)and I have to say that some of the very best times of my life were spent with all of you! Everyone of us are so different in so many ways (in beliefs, in career paths, etc.) and yet we all share a common bond and that is the love that we have for each other and our family. As each of us have grown up and expanded our lives with our own children and grandchildren, this common core of love among us has only increased exponentially! I am so grateful for each and every one of you! You are all wonderful....I just cannot say that enough...

And lastly, I would like to thank my Mom. My Mom is an amazing woman, who I love very much! She is an important part of my life and she is cherished....more than she could ever know or that I could ever explain or put into words.....

CPSIA information can be obtained
at www.ICGtesting.com
Printed in the USA
LVHW031121060521
686680LV00008B/416